KEEPER

OF

CORPSES

AND OTHER DARK TALES

Cassandra O'Sullivan Sachar

VELOX BOOKS
Published by arrangement with the author.

Keeper of Corpses and Other Dark Tales copyright © 2024 by Cassandra O'Sullivan Sachar.

All Rights Reserved.

This book is a work of fiction. People, places, events, and situations are the product of the author's imagination. Any resemblance to actual persons, living or dead, or historical events, is purely coincidental.

No part of this book may be reproduced, stored in a retrieval system, or transmitted by any means without the written permission of the author and publisher.

For Simon.

CONTENTS

Spring

Keeper of Corpses 1

Soothsayer 7

Untenanted 17

Budget Wine Tour 25

And They Marched On 37

Skin Deep 43

Summer

From the Sea to the Sea 51

(In)termina(b)l(e) 57

A Gift for Avery 63

Itch 71

Crawl Space 75

The Mirror 83

The Cigarette-Mouthed Man 89

Tunnel Vision 95

Fall

Matka Loves You 103

Under the Apple Tree 105

Night School 109

Glitch in the System 115

When the Truth Comes Crashing Down 125

Run! 127

House of Screams 137

Winter

Not a Cat Guy 145

Christmas Market Massacre 155

Hungry Christmas 163

Together for Christmas 171

Getaway 175

I'll Sleep Tomorrow 191

Afterword: How I Made the Sausage and Other Spoilers 199

About the Author 205

Publication History 207

SPRING

KEEPER OF CORPSES

I am at peace amongst the dead. They are silent, unlike the living. No longer able to move their lips, the dead cannot fling gibes or barbs. But they talk.

No, not like that—I don't speak to spirits. The dead tell me how they lived their lives, not with words but evidence. Their soft stomachs and flabby thighs grant testament to sedentary living and cheap fast food. Dilated blood vessels, bulbous noses, and jaundiced skin spill the secrets of a heavy drinker. Stained or missing teeth and receding gums suggest a smoker even if I can't detect the stench of nicotine seeped into their skin.

And then there are the scars, marks of pain and life and vanity. Long, straight cuts to reach a heart and keep it pumping; ropy incisions where babies were extracted from wombs; nips and tucks behind ears and under breasts to keep age at bay.

But the years march on, all the same. Time stops for no one, etching itself onto skin, cracking and sagging once-taut flesh. Thick hair ebbs away into wisps; eyes yellow and cloud.

The residents are all old here, at the nursing home. By the time they reach us, if their minds remain intact, they know they have arrived to depart.

I am the keeper of corpses. The other nurses at Blackthorn Manor beckon me when death inevitably calls, and I answer. No one looks for me when they want to gossip, or when relatives visit to coo over a baby. Refusing to call a ninety-year-old "young lady" or inquire about grandchildren as some of the others do, I remain silent, like the dead, and go about my business, providing medication and emptying bed pans. I am not paid for conversation.

Unlike my coworkers, with cartoon characters on their scrubs and forced grins from ear to ear, my life is not measured in carpool lines and soccer games. These women fawn and chat; they are the ones my boss desires to flit around when prospective residents or their families tour the home. They are large and bright and loud where I am small and dark and quiet.

But where my coworkers cry and fret is where I shine. I give the dead the care they need, the respect they deserve.

There is stillness in death. Old Mr. Gruber's arthritic fingers can no longer reach out and pinch my side or grasp my wrist as I remove his IV. I elevate his head onto a clean pillow and place his dentures back in his mouth before livor mortis sets in. Closing his eyes, the ones that used to glare at me as I conducted my work, I place a rolled towel under his chin to shut his mouth.

The funeral home will prepare his body for viewing, but I take care of Mr. Gruber first: bathing him, changing his gown and sheets, combing his hair, removing his socks and tagging his right toe with his identifiers, and placing a fresh pad underneath to help guard for leakage before maneuvering the body bag around him. I had scant affection for Mr. Gruber, with his sharp tongue and searching hands, but I treat his body with respect, as I do with all the corpses I prepare. I zip the bag up over his face, my work completed.

People weep constantly here, the elderly and their loved ones. The sounds of despair pervade the halls. But their deaths no longer move me. To die of old age is a blessing, when one's own body, rather than the evils of the world, is the only force that threatens.

My son will never reach old or even middle age, his life stolen away at nineteen, more boy than man. His murderer walks free.

It was self-defense, the attorney told the jury, his expensive suit and slicked-back hair exuding money and authority. *The deceased had a knife. It's a tragedy, but one young man's life is already gone. How does it right a wrong to destroy the life of another?*

An attempted mugging outside a college party, I was told. The defendant claimed my son drew a knife and asked him and his friend for their wallets, and that what happened next was in self-defense. As if two brawny fraternity boys needed protection from my quiet, slight Angelo, with his long eyelashes and gentle ways.

The defense attorney produced the knife, bagged as evidence. He said my son's fingerprints covered it. But my Angelo, my angel, was not cruel. I begged the judge to examine his spotless record, his letters of recommendation from his high school teachers, his excellent grades at the university. A good boy, he did his chores and said his prayers, back when I believed prayers had value.

He was picked on as a child, teased and taunted at school. *He is a good student*, the teachers told me, *but he does not have any friends.*

Watching and listening to the testimonies, I saw the boys' smirks. Angelo's life was inconsequential to them. They planted the knife in his hand. I know it.

The defendant bloodied his knuckles as he bashed in my sweet son's tender head, so he was the one arrested, later released. When the ambulance arrived for Angelo, it was already too late. His faint pulse expired by the time he reached the hospital.

The policewoman sat me down before she recited the news. Her heavy eyes held only a fraction of the sorrow I would feel when her strangled words emerged.

Is there anyone you can call? she asked after my first wave of sobbing passed. As she peeked at her vacant-eyed male partner, I felt a small comfort it was a woman who told me.

But there was no one who would come. I immigrated here for a better life, for opportunity. I raised my son in this country, alone, his father gone, my parents dead and buried.

When I arrived to identify Angelo's body, that which had grown inside my own, he was already prepared, but poorly. They had taped his eyes shut—*I use moist cotton balls if the eyelids won't cooperate, and try again, so the look is more restful.* Though the nurse had wiped the blood from his bruised, sunken face, ruby specks glittered behind his ears and in the creases of his broken nose. A hasty job, one completed without enough care.

There is nothing we can do, the assistant district attorney told me after the trial. *I'm sorry, but the man who beat your son to death will walk free.*

But I could wait. And I have.

***

Chad Worthington, a name that oozes wealth and privilege, was a football star in college, a beast of a man compared to my slender Angelo. As Angelo has rotted in the ground these past eighteen months, Chad has graduated college and now works at a mortgage company. How I loathe knowing these details of his successful life.

I have watched him, learning his habits, his routine. For months, I have waited outside his workplace and followed him, from a distance, to the various bars he frequents. I keep to myself, ordering a single drink or small plate of food. A chameleon blending into the background, I am small and quiet and remain unseen, wearing hats and sunglasses, wigs and jackets. At times, I wear lifts in my shoes or padding on my body, altering my size, careful not to be recognized.

Tonight I *choose* to be seen. By him, this awful man who took my son.

I dress for Chad to notice. I know his type. A short, tight skirt and push-up bra; a blonde wig. Heavy makeup to slough off years and transform me into another woman. Chad would never recognize me as the bereaved mother from the courtroom whose child he had slain.

Sitting at the bar, I order a glass of white wine and bide my time.

It doesn't take long. Of course it doesn't. I know his style, the way he comes to bars alone and preys on single women.

I flirt. My skin crawls with revulsion, but I giggle and tease and allow his damp, meaty hand to linger on my thigh. Sipping my drink as he guzzles his own, I know that the time has come.

"Let's go back to my place," I whisper in his ear.

Chad is almost too obliging. I convince him not to take his car, for he has had too much to drink. I slide his phone out of his pocket when he isn't looking and leave it on his barstool. I can tell that it's new and expensive, so someone will take it far away. I have read that pinging cellphones can be traced, and I must remain undetectable.

We walk the mile or so to my rowhome. No one notices us, a drunken couple like so many others on this warm spring night, meandering under the drooping limbs of the blossoming magnolias.

It's late, the houses dark, my neighbors sleeping or out of town. Though they don't know me, I pay attention to whose mail is piling up, which cars haven't moved. Timing is everything.

Despite this caution, we enter through the back door, away from streetlights. Chad squeezes and grabs at me, and it is all I can do not to scream. But I have come this far.

Keeping the lights dim, lest my true age reveal itself, I turn on music, something young and suggestive. "Let me get us some drinks," I say, placing a hand on his chest, allowing it to rest a moment.

He sits on the couch, pulsing with anticipation.

***

It was easy to snatch the pain pills from Mr. Gruber's room, a few from different bottles to escape notice, and easier still to crush them with a rolling pin. Glancing into the living room, I stay cautious, but Chad never thinks to check on me while I gather our drinks. I stir the powder in with a straw.

Chad drinks his beer fast, and the pills, combined with the large amount of alcohol he has already imbibed, work their magic. His large frame slumps to the floor. Leaving the music on lest he wake up and yell, I fasten his hands and feet together with zip ties and duct tape his mouth.

I have planned for this. When I moved, I ensured that the house had a dirt floor in the cellar. I have strengthened my muscles, practicing for what I must do.

But first, I prepare. I scrub off my makeup and remove my wig. I want him to recognize me in his final moments. I change out of my tawdry clothes and into a surgical gown and rubber gloves. Dragging him, I allow his head to bump down the stairs, not being careful. Unlike my Angelo, it won't matter if Chad sustains a concussion.

Panting from the exertion of hauling his beefy physique, I prop him upright and tie him with rope to one of the metal columns.

Then I wait for him to awaken, my set of knives at the ready.

***

Does his sin leave his body as I slit his throat? Does it enter my own flesh, for committing this crime? It is no matter. He appears peaceful, now that it's over, the terror leaving as fast as the light in his eyes extinguished. I never asked him why he did it, why he attacked my son and lied.

I begin my preparations to his body. But rather than bathing and bagging him whole, I will sow his parts like seeds in my cellar.

Smiling, I think back to my girlhood at the family farm, when my grandfather demonstrated how to slaughter and dress a pig. With the full weight of my rage, I swing the meat cleaver down across Chad's calf, severing it, flesh and bone. Blood sprays on my gown in a crimson arc.

Sweat drips down my back as I finish my work, the chopping and the planting, like Chad with the knife.

Later, after I rest, I shall bag up the wig and the clothes, mine and Chad's, and drive across and out of town to various receptacles. As a nurse, I know the importance of disposing of biohazardous waste in a proper fashion, sealed and wrapped in plastic bags. I will keep my knives—they are precious to me now.

Next week, I will begin to lay concrete over the dirt floor. Just in case. I have researched how to do this and have purchased the materials.

It feels comforting, having Chad here, a reminder of my vengeance.

I am the keeper of corpses.

SOOTHSAYER

Like vultures, the visions descended, uninvited and impossible to ignore.

The first time it happened, she was nine, playing Barbies with her friend Chloe. As Hannah brushed her doll's long, silky hair, her head filled with the picture of Chloe's dad, a hangdog expression on his face and suitcase in his hand. "Your mom and dad are getting a divorce," Hannah blurted out.

Chloe stared at her, dark eyes flashing. "Why would you *say* that? My parents are fine." She threw the Barbie back into Hannah's bin. "I'm calling my mom to pick me up. I don't want to play with you anymore." She got up fast, long braids whipping around her head.

"Chloe, wait! I didn't mean to make you mad!" Hannah reached out to grasp her friend's shoulder, but Chloe had already run up the basement stairs.

"Ms. McGregor? I need to use your phone, please." Chloe stood in the kitchen, her pose stiff.

Seated at the wooden kitchen table, a mess of bills spread out before her, Hannah's mother glanced back and forth between the two girls. "Is everything okay? What happened?"

Chloe shook her head, her mouth puckered as if she'd been eating Sour Patch Kids. "It's *not* okay. I need to call my mom." Hannah's mom handed over her phone, which Chloe took into the living room for a short, whispered conversation.

Hours later, Hannah's mom knocked on her bedroom door. "Honey, put your book down for a few minutes. We need to talk." She sat on the edge of the bed, next to her daughter, and smoothed down the rainbow comforter. "Chloe and her mom are both upset. I'm not mad at you, but why'd you say that?"

Hannah rolled her eyes. "I *said* it because it's true. I feel bad for Chloe, but she deserves to know. I wasn't trying to be mean. She told you, didn't she? Chloe's mom?"

Her voice gentle, Hannah's mom answered, "Yes, but they hadn't told Chloe yet, and how did you even know?"

Hannah shrugged. "I just knew."

"Did Chloe say her parents were fighting?"

"No, Mom, I just knew, like I know we're having pizza for dinner tonight." She sat up, her hand still on her book, anxious to travel back to Narnia.

"We *always* get pizza on Saturday nights. Did you see something, or hear something, when you were at Chloe's house last weekend? You weren't looking at anyone's phone, were you? You need to respect people's privacy."

"No, Mom, I'm telling you, I just knew that they were getting a divorce. Chloe's dad's gonna move out. It just hasn't happened yet." Hannah raised her gray eyes to her mother's. "And it's not fair that Chloe's mad at me when I'm not even the one doing anything bad to her. She should be mad at her parents, not *me*."

Hannah's mom ran her hand through her hair and rose from the bed. "I'll go order the pizza."

***

Chloe wouldn't talk to Hannah after that. They had to pick partners in gym class the next week, and Hannah headed over, but Chloe had already paired up with Blair, leaving Hannah stuck with Jamie, who smelled like cat pee. If Hannah sat next to her at lunchtime, Chloe got up and moved to another table before Hannah could even offer her some of her Oreos as a peace offering. When Hannah tried to speak with her, to apologize for what she had said, Chloe would look away.

As the weeks wore on, Hannah yearned for her friend. She missed swinging with her at recess and sleeping over on Friday nights, staying up all night watching movies and playing video games. Chloe's dad had moved out by then. It didn't pop into Hannah's head, not like before, but she overheard Chloe telling Blair about it one day at school. "It's like Hannah *made* it happen, like she's a witch."

The words cut into Hannah's heart.

***

The visions kept coming. Sometimes Hannah's foresight was inconsequential, like that the neighbors were getting a new SUV or that her classroom would adopt a rabbit named Pickle. She didn't bother sharing these things with anyone—they didn't really matter. But other times, when she thought she could help, she'd tell.

"You need to slow down today or you're going to get pulled over," she had warned as her dad slugged down his coffee before heading to work. But he didn't listen, and she heard him grumble to her mom about his speeding ticket later that night.

Hannah's mom wouldn't listen, either. "Don't get the shrimp lo mein or you'll get sick," Hannah advised, but her mother ordered it anyway and had to call out of work the next day, hunched over the toilet and puking her guts out.

Her mother had the habit of looking at her sideways when she thought Hannah wouldn't notice. It was right before her tenth birthday, the first year she said she didn't want a party since she figured no one would come, when her mom finally told her to stop.

"You scare people when you say stuff like that," her mother said. "Keep it to yourself, Hannah. You're not helping anyone, especially not yourself. You're never going to make any friends if you say these nasty things."

Hannah's eyes filled with tears. "I'm not saying *nasty* things. I wanna help people." She thought about how she had told the Browns down the street that their dog was going to get hit by a car if they didn't fix the loose board in their fence, and how she told Mrs. Grimes, her teacher, that Johnny Bennett was going to steal her wallet if she kept bringing her purse into the classroom instead of locking it in her car. But the Browns' friendly Collie got hit and killed, his blood staining the street, and the only child who got called into the principal's office when the wallet went missing was Hannah herself.

"I don't want to tell you this again, Hannah," her mother said. "Whatever you're playing at, I don't like it. Neither does your father, or your teacher, or any of our neighbors. Whatever you think you know, keep it to yourself."

So she did, mostly succeeding, but there were times when her conscience wouldn't allow it. Not wanting to upset her mother or add to the rumors that swirled around school about her, she kept her warnings anonymous.

At age twelve, she wrote a note to her principal asking him to please go to the doctor and get his heart checked. He missed a few days of school but kept working long after that, and she didn't have any new visions of him dying of a heart attack, so maybe he listened. He *must've* listened.

If she *told*, if she let people know what might happen to them, she could stop it. Sometimes it worked, and other times it didn't.

At age fourteen, she made a phone call to the local 7-Eleven, telling them to please be careful, maybe even stay closed, on May 29th. She spoke in what she thought sounded like a grownup voice, but the owner, a kind man who always gave Hannah a free donut hole when she was little, swore at her and hung up. The following day, he was shot and killed by an armed robber.

It weighed on her soul, all the things she knew but couldn't tell. But she locked it up inside of herself and tried to go about her business.

Her father, his breath smelling of whiskey, once asked her to tell him what numbers to play in the lottery. "Hannah, you've never been an easy daughter to raise, so do this for us. Do this one thing for your mother and me. *Tell* me."

"I can't, Dad. I'm sorry. It doesn't work that way." That was the truth—she didn't see everything or know everything, only what came to her, and most of it was irrelevant and inconsequential. She couldn't read minds and never had an inkling as to what questions teachers would ask on tests, which might have been helpful, especially in her AP chemistry class. But she was grateful for this, for whatever unknown force funneled away information. It was too much to bear as it was, the apparitions that flooded her thoughts unbidden.

"What use is it having a freak for a daughter if she can't even help us?" he snarled, and Hannah retreated to her room, alone.

Freak. Weirdo. Loser. She'd heard it all over the years. Ever since she'd spilled the beans about Chloe's parents, she'd never had any real friends. Classmates who were too polite to bully her still wouldn't talk to her.

Her dad had a point. Why have this knowledge if almost no one ever listened to her? And she couldn't even help her*self*. Hannah saw the lives of others unfold with crystal clarity, able to make out the O of horror that old Mrs. Carter's mouth formed as she fell down the stairs, but Hannah didn't know to avoid Market Street on the day she got rear-ended driving her mom's car to school senior year. And she certainly didn't know that Brian Jennings had placed the dead rat in her backpack; she'd just walked around as people laughed at her and then screamed in shock when she pulled out her trigonometry textbook and discovered the limp, mangled corpse.

When it was time to apply to college, Hannah chose a small private school in Vermont. If she could get far enough away from Blackthorn, she could start over with no one the wiser. Her parents seemed happy enough to put hundreds of miles between them and their only child.

Over the years, Hannah had developed some coping skills. When a violent image rushed at her—blood splashed on walls and crushed cars and ruined bodies—she stared hard at the most beautiful object she could see with her actual eyes: the delicate pink petals of a rose, or the brilliant red feathers of a cardinal. She counted backward from ten and embraced the sight, trying to shut off the frightful movie projector that played inside her head.

Sometimes it worked, and other times it didn't.

***

Fall descended upon her college campus, and Hannah focused her eyes on a curling orange leaf as she attempted to block out the bruised face of a boy in her anthropology class who would get mugged and savagely beaten when he went home to Philadelphia. She watched the sunset, the pink and yellow hues painting the sky, and tried to close her mind's eye on the vacant, lifeless face of her sociology professor, an older woman who would get hit by a car while running into the street after her escaped cat.

At least she no longer saw the ills that would befall her parents; her gift, her curse, whatever it was, had a limited radius, apparently. On the few occasions she called home, she was blissfully ignorant of their lives, and she rambled on about her classes and college life as if she were normal.

People at college thought she *was* a regular person. When she summoned up the courage to raise her hand in English class, the professor smiled and nodded, complimenting her insight. A classmate in macroeconomics leaned over and asked her to be partners one day. And at lunch early in the semester, a girl from her dorm floor beckoned her over to share their meal together.

Hannah didn't tell anyone what would happen to them. She shut it all away, careful to maintain the illusion that she was like everyone else.

But then she met Lydia.

***

Hannah's roommate Becca played on the field hockey team. Hannah avoided Becca's invitations to frat parties but attended every home game. What might she say if her tongue loosened with alcohol? She couldn't risk *that*, but she supported her roomie by sitting on the sidelines, even though she didn't understand a darn thing about field hockey. Becca had plenty of other friends and didn't need her there, but Hannah enjoyed feeling connected. She swelled with pride whenever Becca scored a goal, shutting out the information that the goalie would get her jaw broken by a stick to the face near the end of the season.

"Hey. Can I sit here?"

Hannah didn't look up, not thinking anyone was speaking to her.

"Hello! Do you mind if I sit with you?"

Hannah slid her eyes to the right and beheld a wide grin under a frizzy mane of dark hair beaming down at her. "Sorry, are you talking to me?"

"Well, yes, you're the only one I see here. I just hate watching sports by myself. So boring, but my roommate's on the team, and I told her I'd come." The girl flopped down on the bleachers beside Hannah, all long, skinny arms and legs like a praying mantis. "You didn't say no, so I'm sitting." She held up her hands in a conciliatory gesture.

"My roommate's on the team, too. That's her—number 14. I'm Hannah."

"Lydia," the girl said, and began rummaging in her bag. To Hannah's delight, she pulled out a bag of kettle corn and a couple of cans of chilled Diet Coke. "I have snacks."

The two girls talked and half-watched the game. It turned out that Lydia was an only child from Pennsylvania, just like her. Lydia set Hannah at ease in a way she hadn't felt since before the visions began plaguing her.

"Give me your phone. We need to hang out again," Lydia commanded as the game ended. "There. Now you have my number. Text me right now so I have yours, too." She waited expectantly as Hannah fumbled.

***

This is my new life, Hannah reminded herself that night as she tried to sleep. *I can have friends. No one knows about me. Just ignore the visions.*

And she did, for a while. She met Lydia for coffee, and she went to her first college party where she drank a beer—just one—encouraged by Lydia's cheers to "let loose." She hung out at Lydia's dorm room when invited and watched scary movies, feeling lighthearted and happy, only inches away from Lydia's warm, prone body.

But, inevitably, she saw Lydia die. In her mind, of course.

***

Should she tell her? Of course she shouldn't tell her. But maybe she could help prevent it from happening. Maybe Lydia, unlike the others, might listen.

The weird part was that she couldn't see Lydia's death scene clearly. The lines of her sight were blurry, as if she were underwater. It might happen years from now, decades. She knew the figure she saw was Lydia—the untamed hair and heavy eyeliner were unmistakable. Hannah noticed that Lydia was wearing a red sweater, but she hadn't seen Lydia ever in that color before, and Hannah always noticed her friend's appearance.

Hannah tried not to worry. But she'd seen Lydia as well as a man in a dark suit, an older man. They were part of a crowd, but Hannah couldn't make out the details of the others. With Lydia and the older man, though, she saw their empty stares, open mouths, and broken bodies.

Hannah couldn't tell Lydia *that.*

***

Winter break came and went, and Hannah traveled back to campus excited to resume her new, normal, happy life. Everything was fine. Until they went shopping, that is.

"I love it. Do you love it? I know it's just a sweater, but I look awesome, right?"

The truth was that Lydia looked beautiful; red complemented her dark hair and olive complexion. But Hannah didn't want her friend to buy the red sweater.

"What about the green? I think that might bring out those specks in your eyes," Hannah said, embarrassed at having noticed but wanting to dissuade Lydia from the purchase without flying her freak flag.

"Nah. Red's a power color. I think I need red. *You* try on the green!" Lydia posed in front of the mirror, and Hannah recalled the fuzzy outline from her mind's eye of Lydia in that same sweater.

***

Hannah knew that Lydia cared about her, though she wasn't sure how much or in what way. Maybe Lydia trusted her enough by now, after all this time, that she'd listen, that she'd throw away that damned red sweater, that she'd save herself from the misfortune that would befall her. *Maybe I should take that red sweater and burn it.*

When Lydia finally showed up at her dorm room in the red sweater, Hannah resigned herself to finally warn her. She just needed the right moment.

"What do you want to do today?" Hannah asked. They didn't always make concrete plans, but Lydia had gotten into the habit of expecting that Hannah would be up for something. She didn't really have any other real friends, after all, so she was available.

"Let's get breakfast and then go to the library to do homework," Lydia said, her voice husky. Hannah hadn't hung out with her the night before since she'd been working on her English essay, but she could tell that Lydia had been smoking cigarettes and probably drinking, too. Not that Hannah judged her.

On alert, Hannah tried to scrounge up the details of what she'd seen in her mind's eye months ago. Red sweater, check. The older guy in the dark suit. Their lifeless, blood-spattered faces.

But that could be years from now. Sweaters lasted forever. Hannah's mom still wore one that she'd bought in college.

After breakfast, they trekked across campus to the library. Hannah headed to the stairs, as always.

"Ugh, come on. I'm stuffed from those waffles and scrambled eggs. I swear I'll work out later. Give me a break." Lydia grabbed Hannah's hand and pulled her toward the elevator.

Hannah didn't use elevators much. She wanted to be healthy. But it was fine. She didn't want Lydia to think she was being weird.

Lydia pressed the button, and the girls waited, Lydia in her red sweater. A few people gathered around them.

Hannah saw the older man in a dark suit from the corner of her eye. Alarm bells went off in her head as she thought about Lydia's red sweater and *this* man in *this* suit.

The elevator opened its doors. Hannah's legs stayed planted on the floor.

"Hannah, come on," Lydia urged, wrenching her arm. "What's wrong with you?"

"No." It was all Hannah could muster. "Stairs. Too crowded." She spoke in staccato, the dread rising in her throat like bile.

"Ladies, let's go. I need to meet my study group." Some guy pushed them from behind, his palms on the smalls of their backs, and Lydia and Hannah were swallowed into the elevator. The heat of strangers' bodies pressed against Hannah through her clothing, onto her skin, yet she shivered.

Lydia reached through the throng and pressed number seven for the floor with their favorite study room in the narrow but tall library.

Hannah held her breath as she ascended. It was *fine*. She hadn't envisioned anything about an elevator. They moved up from the ground floor to one, two, and three, the chime dinging but no one getting out.

At four, the frat-looking guy who'd pushed them in and some others walked out, but the older man in the dark suit stayed put. It was still crowded in the tight space.

As the doors closed, Hannah's vision returned, but the blurriness had dissipated. That's when she saw herself standing in an elevator with Lydia and the older man.

This elevator.

She'd never seen herself in a vision, but there she was. And she knew what was coming.

Hannah clamored to push her way past the bodies, to press the emergency buttons, but it was too late.

When the elevator approached the sixth floor, the cable snapped with a roar. As the chamber fell fast down the shaft, Hannah had only a few seconds of her life left to think about how she could have stopped all this.

Sometimes it worked, and other times it didn't.

UNTENANTED

When Hailey Abbot was six years old, she discovered she could leave her body.

Stuck at the fabric store with her mother instead of curled up on the couch watching Saturday morning cartoons with her dog, Hailey was miserable. She *hated* fabric stores, hated how her mother spent hours caressing the brightly-colored bolts beneath her finger tips.

"We'll just pop in and out," her mother would say, but then she'd start conversations about quilting techniques with ladies in the store, and Hailey would end up sitting on the dusty linoleum for hours on end, aching to leave. She didn't know what a Crazy Nine Patch pattern was and didn't care about backing versus basting—it was *so* boring.

Staring at her own open-eyed body propped against a set of shelves in the flannel section, she figured she had fallen asleep.

But Hailey could see everything around her clearly—it wasn't like her regular dreams, where objects looked fuzzy, as if she were wearing goggles. She even noticed a fleck of dried ketchup on her other self's chin. When she rubbed her own face, she felt the dry, flaky texture.

It seemed wrong, somehow, seeing herself this way. She searched for her mother at the back of the store, still chatting away.

Hailey knew she wasn't supposed to interrupt when grownups were talking, but she did it anyway, wanting the creepy feeling to go away. "Are you almost done, Mom?"

But her mother kept talking like she wasn't even there. Hailey reached for her sleeve but watched her fingers slither right through.

Her chest tightened, as if she were underwater and needed to come up for air. She felt a pulling sensation, a frantic tug to her other self. Hailey allowed herself to be dragged back to the flannel section and poured into her body like pancake batter onto a griddle.

She opened and closed her fist, making sure both selves were together as one. "Mom?"

Her voice, loud and quavering, must have indicated her distress, for Hailey's mother rushed to her side. Crouching on her knees, frowning, she felt Hailey's forehead. "Are you okay, honey? You look pale."

Hailey was a good girl who tried to tell the truth. But when she opened her mouth, all she said was, "I think I need to eat something."

On the car ride home, belly full of ice cream, Hailey thought about what had happened and decided she couldn't tell, even though it scared her. *Especially* because it scared her.

★★★

The next time Hailey left her body, she was in third grade, taking an oral spelling test and trying to picture the word "homonym." Her teacher, Miss Goldstein, had a poster behind her desk with that word written on it, but Hailey couldn't see it in her mind's eye.

Then there she was, staring at it.

Hailey flushed red, waiting for the teacher's reprimand for getting up during a test and cheating, but Miss Goldstein simply gave the next word, "repetition." Hailey's other self sat at her desk, unmoving, not writing a word.

She didn't want Miss Goldstein to notice. She rushed back into her body and resumed her exam.

★★★

By middle school, Hailey had learned some control. Though she still slipped out of her body accidentally at times, often when distracted or upset, she could now leave at will. But she remained careful.

Once, she had gone wandering—for that's what she called it—while watching television with her mother. She knew no one could see or hear her, and she had built up endurance to go for longer times and farther distances from her body. She passed through the door and glided down the street, moving lighter and more gracefully than when in her body.

She watched the late summer sunset, appreciating the creamy sherbet colors bleeding into each other, before heading back inside.

But when she reentered the house, her mother's screams filled the room. She jumped back into her body.

"Mom! Stop! What are you doing?" Hailey wrenched her mother's arms away.

"Hailey! I thought you were dead! I called 911!" Her mother spoke into the phone: "She's okay—I don't know what happened. Yes, yes, I will follow up with the doctor."

"I'm fine. I must've fallen asleep."

"Your eyes were open. They were about to have me do mouth to mouth!" With her mother's face a tearstained mask of anguish, Hailey's guilt consumed her.

From then on, she limited her wandering—she'd leave her room with the door locked and music playing. If her mother knocked on the door, she'd have a few minutes' leeway to say she hadn't heard her, an interlude to do whatever she wanted with no one the wiser.

***

Hailey's power enthralled her. Sashaying outside in the dead of winter in her pajamas, she didn't feel cold when wandering and left no footsteps in snow. Nighttime was best, for her mother was less prone to check on her, and Hailey adored watching the nocturnal creatures: the deer, guileless to any presence, munching away on the grass while the wolf stayed in the shadows under the moonlit sky, waiting for the opportunity to begin his hunt. Only Hailey, undetected, could view nature's majesty this way.

She stayed away longer and longer, heading back when her lungs started begging for air and the tide pulled her back to her body.

Hailey wondered if there was some great purpose as to why she could come and go as she pleased, a reason she could shed her flesh like a winter coat, but she had no insight and no one to talk to. Her wandering was just something she could do, like how some people could wiggle their ears. She gave up questioning and focused on enjoying her secret.

Until she was caught.

***

The Russos lived a few doors down from the Abbots' house. Hailey wasn't really listening when her mother told her about the elder Mrs. Russo moving in. Hailey had babysat for the family a few times, but little Charlie threw terrible tantrums, so she pretended to be busy unless in dire need of cash.

As Hailey sailed through the neighborhood over a sea of fallen leaves one autumn evening, the old lady standing on the lawn seemed to look straight at her. By now, Hailey was accustomed to this discomfort—she didn't bat an eyelid.

"I see you, Hailey Abbot," Mrs. Russo's voice, full of gravel and razor blades, reverberated out to her.

Hailey slid to a halt. How did this woman know her name? Better yet, how could she *see* her?

"You can see me? Can you *hear* me?" Hailey approached with caution; she couldn't believe it, not after all of these years going unnoticed.

"Clear as daylight. Better than my ruined eyes can see from my actual body." She gestured toward the house with her thumb. "I'm inside, lying in my hospital bed. Now that I can't walk, can't do anything, really, I like getting outside for a change of scenery and to pretend I can breathe this fresh air. Meanwhile, my earthly lungs are chock full of fluid."

Hailey gaped at her. There was so much to ask; she wanted to feast on the old woman's wisdom like it was a big, thick steak.

"Cat got your tongue, girl? If you've got something to say, out with it. I don't know how much longer I have."

Hailey didn't know if Mrs. Russo meant she'd need to go back to her body soon, or if she was suggesting that she was dying. She didn't want to be insensitive, but she wanted more information from this single person who could understand her gift. "You wander, Mrs. Russo?"

"Ever since I was a girl. But I call it traveling. And call me Agnes." She smiled, eyes gleaming. "You?"

"Since I was six." Hailey started blurting it all out to this stranger, spilling the secrets she had kept, from the first time in the fabric store to her longer and more recent trips, nearly twelve years later. She said so much so fast that she almost didn't notice the familiar feeling, the constricted lungs and wrenching back to her body.

Agnes knew. Of course she did. "Young lady, this has been a pleasant gab session, but I can tell you need to go. Tomorrow, same time, same place?"

Hailey nodded, regretting how she had monopolized their conversation, wishing she had asked Agnes about her own experiences.

***

They met the next day, and the next, and Hailey remembered to listen rather than share. Agnes understood Hailey's need for guidance.

"Look, sister, I'll tell you what I know. I've been traveling for seventy-odd years, but the doctor says my days are numbered. Somebody might as well benefit from all this knowledge. If that person is you, and I can help you, great."

Agnes told stories about leaving her body for hours on end, giving Hailey tips on building up strength so she could do it, too. She regaled Hailey with tales of going backstage with the Beatles and standing by as Queen Elizabeth ate her dinner.

"I had to haul my earthly body to England first, but the sky's the limit once you park your carcass near Buckingham palace. I boogied right past those guards with their big, silly hats. I had a ball." Agnes sighed, a small smile playing on her lips. "What I wouldn't give to be in your shoes now, ready to start your journey."

Alive with possibility, Hailey planned events in her future. As soon as she graduated from Blackthorn High next month, before she started college, she could do whatever she liked. What great fun it would be, enjoying life in a way almost no one else could. Following Agnes's example, she could go anywhere, do anything: walk through every velvet rope to the most exclusive celebrity parties if she wanted, or maybe slide down Niagara Falls or the Grand Canyon.

One day, at their normal meeting time, Agnes wasn't waiting for her.

Panic coursed through Hailey's veins. Had she passed? Agnes had said she wasn't long for this world.

Hailey didn't want to intrude, but she peeked into the Russos' house to check if her friend was okay. There lay Agnes in the hospital bed, looking so much weaker and smaller than how Hailey knew her. Her eyes, cloudy with glaucoma, were open, but Hailey knew her friend was still alive—the machine at her bedside registered a weak heartbeat.

If Agnes was out wandering, where had she gone? She was always there for Hailey. They were there for each other, the only two people who understood this special talent.

Hailey left the Russos' and searched the neighborhood. Maybe Agnes was out on a nature walk. But she couldn't find her anywhere.

Her chest burning, Hailey headed home, saddened by the lack of connection. She passed through her front door and into her bedroom, anxious to get back into her body.

But her body was no longer lying in bed. Instead, Hailey gasped in horror to see herself sitting at her desk, laptop open to a travel site, singing along with Spotify to "Hey, Jude."

Hailey tried to climb back into this moving, blinking being, *her* body, but there was no room. Though her lungs gulped for air, Hailey realized she wasn't feeling the gravitational tug to come back to her body.

Instead, she was pulled away, in another direction. Weak with betrayal, she let the current drag her in—she knew where she was headed. She just needed to breathe, and she'd come back to claim what was rightfully hers. *Her* body. *Her* life.

Down the street she soared, through the front door of the Russos' house.

She had no choice. She climbed into the atrophied figure stretched out on the bed, desperate to release the pressure in her lungs.

Hailey waited for the heaviness to abate, but, if anything, it had grown. She took deep, gasping breaths, unable to escape the vice clamping her chest.

"Help me," she croaked.

Mr. Russo rushed in and grasped her hand, a shriveled, veiny claw.

"Mom, I'm here. The doctor said it won't be long now. You'll be at peace."

Hot tears leaked out of eyes that were not hers, and the thin chest that was not Hailey's moved up and down, up and down, and finally stopped.

BUDGET WINE TOUR

Clara scrolled through excursions on her phone before tossing it on the bed and burying her face in the thin hotel pillow. "Everything's *so expensive*."

"We didn't come all the way to Chile to stay in our hotel room every night. You really can't find *anything* in our budget?" Derek wasn't as worried about money as his wife. After merging their bank accounts together when they got married the previous year, he was content for her to take control of the finances: checking the balance, paying the bills, and figuring out how much they could afford on expenditures like evenings out and vacations. While grateful for the way Clara had whipped their savings account into much better shape than in his bachelor days, he hated penny-pinching and missed the freedom of blowing a hundred dollars at the bar on a night out with friends.

"Derek, think about all that we spent already." There were the extra baggage fees even though they'd taken the cheapest flight they could find, plus the added surprise of mandatory travel health insurance before they could enter the country. This ate into the money they'd saved for entertainment, so they'd already found a grocery store to buy granola bars and sandwiches to make up for it, walking past the slew of restaurants with their enticing live music and savory, tantalizing aromas.

"Didn't you say it was a dream of yours to go on a wine tour in South America?" Their favorite brand of wine back home, a $5 steal at the budget liquor store, hailed from the very region they were visiting. One tipsy night, satiated with Sauvignon Blanc, Clara had confessed this desire, and Derek brought it out now not to manipulate but to lure. Besides, if he got the promotion to manager he was expecting, their days of living on the cheap would ease up. Clara had grown up poor, so even with their comfortable paychecks, Derek had to assure her that they could still pay their mortgage. Then again, she was an accountant, so she always knew exactly where they stood.

Clara sat up, retrieving her phone, a smirk playing on her lips. "Well, there was this *one* ad I found, but I've never heard of the travel company, and they didn't have any reviews."

"It's not like we're seasoned travelers. Who cares if we've heard of them?" Derek took a moment to browse the pictures and offering. "This looks amazing. Tour in English, tastings and tapas, and they pick us up from the hotel, all for $75 each? Babe, this sounds like a good deal. Let's do it."

The tight set of Clara's jaw loosened, her eyes opening wide to show that flash of madness when she broke out of the control she exerted over herself. She grabbed her phone back and started typing. "Okay! Done. We're leaving at 10 a.m. tomorrow morning."

***

A black luxury car pulled up in front of their shoddy hotel. When a slight man in a black suit, a proper chauffeur, climbed out, Derek was sure this car wasn't for them.

"Derek and Clara?" the man asked.

The couple exchanged a look. *This* was the budget wine tour?

"Yes, that's us. I mean, *si, Señor*." Derek shifted, uncomfortable in his embarrassing lack of Spanish, wishing he had taken advantage of that Duolingo app his sister had suggested.

"My name is Carlos, and I speak a little English. Please excuse my mistakes," Carlos said perfectly while ushering them into the backseat.

They spent a contented hour or so in the sedan watching the landscape transform from graffiti-encrusted buildings to lush, rolling hills and verdant pastures. Every now and then, Clara pointed out grazing horses or sheep. Derek sensed his wife's happiness at this South American adventure and was glad he had championed this vacation rather than embark on another free but predictable trip to his parents' cabin in the Poconos.

"We're almost there!" Clara's eyes were glued to the window as she imbibed the rows of vine-covered trellises. "Oh my God, it's amazing. I'm so, so excited we came here." She clasped Derek's hand.

They pulled into the wide gravel driveway toward a grand white edifice with arched windows and balconies. A tall, slim man in a tie and tweed sports jacket stood outside, waiting.

"Welcome to Bodega Toro Negro," Carlos intoned, stopping the car. "Today you will have a private tour given by the winemaker and owner himself, Eduardo. I hope you will enjoy your time at this beautiful vineyard."

"*Muchas gracias*," Derek said. He let out a low whistle. "I'm feeling pretty boujie, babe. A private tour with the winemaker, all for $75 each? This is the deal of a lifetime."

"Welcome!" Eduardo called out, moving closer to his guests and extending long, slender fingers. "I am Eduardo. I am so pleased to invite you into my home today as my honored guests. This is a special day, and we are most delighted with your arrival. We will start with a tour of the grounds, and then we will visit the cellar, where I will tell you about the process and show you how our wine is made. Next, you will enjoy a tasting of Bodega Toro Negro's finest wines paired with Chilean cuisine. I believe you will find this most satisfactory." He smiled, exposing two straight rows of gleaming white teeth.

"Chilean wine dates back to the 16th century, with the Spanish conquistadors, but it is quite new to this area, the Casablanca Valley," Eduardo continued. "My family has owned this estate for several generations, since 1875, but we have only been making wine since my childhood. We grew wheat for over one hundred years, yet my grandfather's poor management of the farm and the finances drove the family to near ruin. When this region exploded into the wine industry in the 1980s, my family decided to take the chance with everything we had left. There were lean years as my parents and aunts and uncles labored to grow the vines and learn the business, but you can see that our fortune has improved. We worked hard, like bulls, and went through great sacrifice." He waved his hand around at the landscape, picturesque and thriving under the endless blue sky.

"It's beautiful," Clara gushed.

Even Derek's imagination was piqued, and he pictured a young Eduardo helping his family through the hardship, planting vines and coaxing them to grow.

"You would normally see many other tourists in the vineyard, but today, this last Sunday of May, is a special day for my family. We are fully closed on Christmas and Easter, but on this family holiday we like to provide one lucky pair of tourists a private tour—whoever is first to claim it on the internet. Today, you are special guests of my family. This is the day we give thanks to the land that has taken care of us. Come, let me teach you about Bodega Toro Negro."

***

The trio walked through the vineyard, stopping every now and then when Eduardo requested that they feel the texture of the soil or the leaves on a vine, pointing out the different varieties of grapes and explaining the types of wine they made. "It is our autumn now in Chile, so our harvest season is done," he informed his guests, showing them the browning leaves. He took them to the converted barn, pointing out the winery equipment, from the press to the fermentation tubs to the gleaming steel casks. Stacked up in pyramids against the walls, the barrels bore stamps with the winery's logo and held around three hundred bottles of wine apiece.

Clara asked a number of questions to which Eduardo responded, but Derek zoned out—he appreciated the science and the effort it took to make wine, but he felt sleepy after being out in the sun and was looking forward to actually *drinking* the wine.

Eduardo must have noticed Derek's glazed eyes as he finished discussing the different information given on each wine barrel. "Come, you have learned enough for now. Now it is time for the tasting!" Eduardo patted Derek on the back and led the way to the white building where Carlos had dropped them off.

They walked through the arched doorway to a shop packed with shelves and display racks with multi-colored bottles, wine openers, glasses, and coasters. A large, unmanned wooden bar dominated the space. "This is where we have our tastings on other days, but you are here for the special tour! I will take you to the cellar." Eduardo gestured to a narrow stairwell.

Derek felt the temperature drop as they descended into the bowels of the building. "It's chilly down here," he said, zipping up his light jacket as they entered the opening, a cave-like dwelling filled with large clay casks, dozens more wine barrels, and a nook where a dinner table and chairs waited, presumably, for them.

"This is where we preserve our most special wine. Heat is the enemy of wine. At this time of year, our cooling system is free of charge for us." Eduardo's thin lips curled into a smile.

Derek wondered about this man, if he were genuinely excited to show off his family business, or if this tour was an annoyance and inconvenience to him. He considered asking how much money the winery made to justify the enormous quantity of inventory they kept, but he didn't want to be a tacky American. His stomach grumbled; they'd been touring for at least two hours now, and it was well past lunchtime.

Eduardo clapped his hands. "My guests, prepare yourselves for the grand finale! It is now time to sample the wares. Please, come sit." He gestured to the long mahogany table under a trellis with fairy lights. It could have easily sat twelve people, but it was set with only two places, each with gleaming plates and cutlery as well as a quartet of differently-shaped wine glasses.

"It's breathtaking," Clara said. "Is all this *really* just for us?"

"You are my honored guests," Eduardo replied, pulling out Clara's chair for her.

A woman appeared as if from nowhere; Derek hadn't heard the patter of her feet on the stairs, but there she was in front of them, holding a bottle of wine out to Eduardo. "Our first wine is a charming Sauvignon Blanc," he began, brandishing the bottle and showing off the black bull on the label.

He went on and on, something about citrus and the pale color, but Derek was beginning to feel irritable, so he picked it up and downed the pour as soon as it reached his glass. He felt a sharp pain on his ankle, a little kick from his wife who hadn't touched her own drink and was regarding him with a steely-eyed glare.

"I will give you the beginner's course to appreciating wine," Eduardo went on, proceeding to explain three steps he called seeing, smelling, and sipping. Clara nodded, listening intently, and Derek followed her lead after his own glass was refurbished. He took it slower this time and was so well-behaved and attentive that he didn't even notice the woman had returned until a platter of olives, bread, nuts, cheese, and empanadas appeared in front of him.

"Sample the gouda with this wine," Eduardo continued, explaining something about the acidity of the wine balancing the buttery cheese. All Derek knew was that he was hungry and everything tasted great. While Clara sipped and nibbled, immersed in the winery's magic, Derek was starving, wanting to guzzle the wine and shovel in the food.

Eduardo moved on to the next sample. "A classic chardonnay, but here at Bodega Toro Negro I believe we have something special. Ours is oak-aged and medium-bodied with tropical flavors. Smell it. Does anything stand out?"

Derek stuck his nose in the glass, trying to concentrate. It smelled like *wine* to him.

"Do I detect a hint of mango?" Clara asked.

"Yes! Very good, Clara!" Eduardo beamed as Derek wondered if there would be more snacks. He gulped his wine and patted his wife's hand to show how impressed he was.

On and on they went, Derek drinking and eating, Clara soaking up all the knowledge she could about the wine. Derek thought the winery was cool and all, but this charcuterie BS wasn't cutting it for a meal. He was anxious to get back to Santiago and get a burger or something. He stifled a yawn, not wanting to be rude, but he'd had a decent amount of wine to drink by this time with Eduardo's generous and frequent pours.

"That was our final wine for this tasting. I hope this has been a pleasant outing for you, yes?" Eduardo asked. "It is of great importance that our special guests learn about the wine and enjoy the day."

"Eduardo, thank you so much. This experience has been transformative for me. I will always carry it with me, this visit to this very special place," Clara said, placing her hand on Eduardo's forearm. Her face had pinkened and her words came out slightly slurred, showing she must have become a little tipsy, even though she'd probably only had about a glass or so of wine altogether.

"Yes. It's been awesome learning about wine culture," Derek said, feeling the need to contribute something. Another massive yawn overtook his body. "Excuse me. I think I may have enjoyed it a little too much."

Clara reached for him, her face contorted into a scowl, likely embarrassed at his gauche behavior, but she staggered. "I'm feeling dizzy," she said, right before she collapsed onto the cellar floor.

"Clara!" Derek called, but his voice sounded far away, like he was stuck in a tunnel, and his world went black.

***

As Derek came to, he was aware of two things: his head hurt, and his body felt constricted. He opened his eyes but saw only darkness. Cognizant of an itch on his head, he tried to scratch it but realized he could not move his arms. Where *was* he? Where was his wife? "Clara?" he called, his voice raspy.

"Ah, you are back with us. The sedative has worn off." Dim light filled the space as Eduardo lifted something from above Derek's head. "There you are! I hope you are not uncomfortable. We like to keep our special guests satisfied until we can no longer do so."

As the light filtered in and his eyes adjusted, Derek peered up at his tour guide and those luminous teeth.

"Breathe in deeply. What do you smell? There will be no more tastings, but, please—inhale the aroma. Do you smell the black cherry? This barrel held a 2018 Cabernet Sauvignon. Now it holds *you*!" Eduardo cackled.

Derek was in no mood for jokes; his brain fought to process the shift from enjoyable wine tour to—what? Kidnapping? He thrashed about in his containment, but his hands and feet were fastened together with plastic zip ties, rendering him immobile. He moved side to side, rocking the barrel, hoping to knock it over. "Let me out!"

"I am so sorry, but we will only be able to let you out later, when it is time. The tradition is to keep our honored guests in the very barrels from which we stored the wine grown by the grapes of this land."

"What tradition are you *talking* about? Is this some kind of prank? And where the hell is my wife?"

"Derek?" Clara's voice, weak and tear-filled, called out from nearby. "Derek? I'm scared!"

"I'll get us out of here, babe! I swear to God!" Derek felt the rage boiling under his skin, the vein pulsing in his temple along with the throbbing of his head. "Eduardo, what in the actual *fuck* are you doing to us?"

"It is difficult to explain in English. But, since you are our special guests, I will try for you," Eduardo began, his voice as calm and collected as when he had described the winemaking process. "You see, my family has struggled. The land can be cruel and refuse to grant us rain to grow our crops. Our land has thrived only when we honor the ancient ways of our ancestors." He paused. "My grandfather, a weak and spineless man, refused to practice the custom, and my family lost almost everything. It was only when my father resurrected the ritual that we had good rain for healthy crops. We are the most prosperous winery in Casablanca Valley! We pay tribute to the land with one man and one woman on this most special Sunday, the last one of May, each year."

"Are you saying you're going to *sacrifice* us? Like, a human sacrifice? You can't do that!" Clara's tinny voice cried out.

Derek felt a great pain in his chest at his wife's distress. All he had wanted was to make her happy. Beneath Eduardo's grinning face and suave clothing, Derek realized, hid pure evil. Bound as he was and disoriented from whatever drugs he had consumed, Derek was helpless. All he could do was try to reason with this lunatic. "Look, man. Okay, you want your winery to be productive. But someone will *notice* if my wife and I disappear. The driver, Carlos, will come back for us, and even if he doesn't, the cops will track our phones. And the woman who fed us—she knows we were here, too. You'll go *down* for this."

"Oh, *Señor*, you must think this is my first final Sunday of May! Do you mean Carlos, my cousin, and Valentina, my sister, who are ready to participate in the ceremony? And do you mean the phones that Carlos took from your sleeping bodies and drove back to a dangerous area of Santiago? Do you mean *those* people and *those* phones? This is not—how do you Americans say it?—my first rodeo. Surely, you cannot imagine we could do this all these years and remain unable to outsmart the *policía*."

Shit. "Yeah, well, they'll track our credit card and internet search history and see that we came here, and when they look back at other American couples who disappeared, they'll see that we all went to this winery before we went missing. Drug us again if you want, drop us off at our hotel, and we'll just be glad we get to live. Do the right thing, man."

"Oh, *Señor*, surely you jest. Tourists disappear all the time. There is no record of you purchasing a tour here—it is an untraceable dummy site, created and already deleted by my cousin Sofia, a genius. And we don't limit ourselves to Americans! We host nearly twenty thousand tourists per year. Tourists from all countries *love* us! We do not discriminate in whom we choose as our special guests—we only require that they speak Spanish or English so *I* can give the tour. I have employees fluent in German, French, Russian, and Italian, but only my *family* may come to Bodega Toro Negro on the night we entertain our *special* guests." He turned away from Derek. "Carlos, last year's guests were Colombian, yes? Marcella and Alejandro, I believe?"

"Yes. Very nice people. The wine has been good this year," Carlos answered. Derek couldn't see him, but he sounded close.

"*Gracias*, Carlos. I agree—they were good people who have helped our wine. You see, my friends, your bodies will calm the land and feed our vines. When we have good people, our wine is better. Even my grandfather and grandmother, my own flesh and blood, have fed the vines. *Abuelo* did not believe in sacrificing others, so my family knew it was time for him and my sweet *abuela* to give back to their land. It was a lovely ceremony, my very first."

He helped kill his own grandparents, and he has no remorse. Derek shuddered, waiting for a miracle, some deus ex machina to save Clara and him from their fate. Yet, there was nothing.

"But it is getting so late! We must begin the ceremony soon. See you in the vineyard!" With that, Eduardo replaced the lid onto the barrel, surrounding Derek in darkness and despair.

This was *real*. This was *happening*, and there was nothing Derek could do about it.

***

Derek heard the grunts of several people, along with Clara's sobs, as their barrels were loaded into some sort of elevator and taken up to the ground floor. From there, they were hoisted onto something else.

"Derek, I think you may have enjoyed too many of our delicious cheeses and empanadas today. You are quite heavy," Eduardo said. "I am kidding! I am happy your final day could be a pleasant one and that you have enjoyed yourself at Bodega Toro Negro."

He could tell they were outside due to the frigid temperature and sounds of the night: an owl hooting in the distance; the lonesome cry of a wolf or coyote. Derek didn't know which species lived in Chile, and now he never would, not that that was his biggest concern. From the inside of his barrel, he was jostled about as the cart rolled over rocks for several minutes before coming to an abrupt halt. A sudden rush of warmth and smell of smoke engulfed him, and Derek could tell they were near a fire.

Eduardo spoke in a flurry of Spanish that Derek didn't understand, and, despite his predicament, he wished he had prepared better for the language requirement of this trip.

"Don't worry, Derek and Clara. I will translate for you. As a final mark of respect to you both for your sacrifice, I would like you to understand. I will begin in Spanish and follow up in English." Eduardo paused, cleared his throat, and resumed, his voice powerful in the stillness of night. "We have reached our clearing. It is almost midnight on the final Sunday of May, and we must pay our respects to the land, to our ancestors, to the vines. First, my family will don our ceremonial garb and each light a candle to honor this tradition."

The group began some sort of low chant which Eduardo didn't translate. It didn't sound to Derek like Spanish, though—it seemed more primitive.

"With this knife, we, the family, will cut our palms and let our blood seep into this earth that has cared for us. We are a part of this land, as you, Derek and Clara, our honored guests, will soon be as well."

Another pause and some murmuring.

"Now, Derek and Clara, I address you directly. Thank you for joining us at our winery today. You shall be a part of our family history now as we plant you in the earth. By the time of our next harvest, your bodies will have fed our vines and sated the land. Our wine will be better with your help. Ladies first!"

Derek couldn't see from the inside of his barrel, but he heard the thud as one of the family members pushed over Clara's barrel. Her muffled cries turned to shrieks of horror.

"Your turn!" Eduardo shouted, and someone gave Derek's barrel a hefty shove. From the glow of the bonfire, he could see the open grave as he tumbled into it, a great gullet chiseled out of the earth, ready to swallow.

He landed in a heap next to his wide-eyed, terrified wife. "I love you, Clara. I'm so sorry I couldn't save us," Derek said, his voice hollow. He looked up at his killers: Carlos, their dapper chauffeur; Eduardo, their garrulous tour guide; Valentina, their quiet server; and four or five others, all of whom wore cloaks of black and held their candles.

They shoveled the soil over his face again and again. Knowing it was hopeless, Derek coughed and sputtered to prevent the dirt from filling his lungs, but it kept coming, returning him to darkness as it covered his eyes. Before he managed his last breaths of air in this final resting place with his beloved, Derek wished he had gotten Clara to agree to a pricier tour.

AND THEY MARCHED ON

Vanessa trudged along, though her limbs protested. She had no choice, having been swept away with the crowd. Her body no longer her own, she was consumed into the jaws of the night, all semblance of her former self and life evaporated.

The hotel clerk had told them to come back before dark. If only she'd listened.

***

10 hours earlier

Paul picked at the loose skin on his lip, a nervous habit exacerbated by the powerful Bolivian sun. Even though it was barely in the 60s, it felt warmer—the sunshine refused to relent, drying out their lips and painting a stinging, rosy burn across their faces. Vanessa had checked her weather app, of course, but hadn't thought to bring sunscreen on their trip.

"It's fine," Vanessa said in response to Paul's unasked question. "I think it'll be interesting."

After the woman at the front desk of the hotel told them that La Paz would celebrate a festival that day, Vanessa's back and neck cramped with the knowledge that the already crowded city would explode. And since their daytrip out of La Paz wasn't scheduled until the following day, *this* Saturday was reserved for spending time in the city.

They ate their breakfast in near silence, milky eggs and thick, viscous coffee that Vanessa needed to dilute with water, and watched the live coverage—in Spanish, of course—on television.

"We can stay in, if you want. I think they have Netflix here," Paul offered.

Vanessa blinked her eyes, considering. After the harrowing journey just to get there, with all the paperwork, fees, and surprise documentation despite having done her homework, and then the minor altitude sickness, another day in the hotel being lazy sounded heavenly. However, she had told Paul she was up for an adventure. She hadn't paid all that money and come all this way to sit in her hotel room, even if that's what she wanted. "Nonsense," she responded, cool and collected, the Vanessa she tried so hard to project to the world instead of the scared rabbit who wanted to cower in the face of adversity. "Let's go explore La Paz!"

***

At first, they *wanted* to be a part of the action. "I don't understand why they've blocked everything off," Paul complained. "It's annoying." Though they'd enjoyed an unencumbered view of the dancers on TV earlier, they could hardly catch a glimpse—thick, blue canvas covered the sides of the bridge and blocked the main streets. "Why would they go to all this trouble to have the festival if they didn't want us to see it?"

"Maybe they want us to pay?" Vanessa saw a line of people stretching out in front of them and could only surmise the reason.

"Let's keep going." Paul grabbed her hand to pull her through the crowd, but Vanessa let her fingers slip away. It was too constricting to walk as a pair amongst the throng of bodies pummeling and pounding her from every direction. Paul knew how Vanessa could be—he said he loved her despite her "difficulties"—but she often wondered if he really, truly understood how hard it was to exist as herself in this inhospitable world where she never seemed to have enough room. Her head pounding with the bang of the drums and gongs, she closed her eyes for a moment, took a deep breath, and placed one foot in front of the other.

***

They stopped for a late lunch at a café. Vanessa melted into the hard, wooden chair, enjoying the luxury of space and air around her.

"Who knew we'd be so lucky to have a free day here during this festival!" Seeming to forget that he had Vanessa for a girlfriend, Paul rambled on and on about the dancers' brightly colored costumes and the jovial atmosphere.

He didn't understand Vanessa's fear of crowds—how they threatened to devour her whole, how her insides felt like they would burst through her skin as strangers pressed into her flesh, how all the light and oxygen depleted for her. This was their first trip outside the country together, and Vanessa had kept it pretty simple for her boyfriend: She didn't like confined spaces. But she hadn't explained the profundity of her affliction.

As Vanessa had fought to keep the panic at bay, focusing on breathing and staying calm, Paul had busied himself taking in all the sights, sounds, and smells as exotic fanfare and exhilaration.

"I mean, this is so different from anything back home. It's so cool! I can't wait to tell the guys about it." He stopped talking to grin at her, but he hadn't finished chewing, and a wet piece of beef from his empanada dangled from his lower lip in the place he had bloodied it earlier.

Vanessa's stomach flipped, and she pushed her plate away, returning his smile weakly. Despite the oasis of this comfortable café, it was only a stopgap until they headed outside into chaos once again. She could no longer bear the thought or aroma of food, which, along with a building headache, nauseated her. She yearned for the day to pass so they could begin their trip to the Uyuni Salt Flats with the wide, open spaces and unusual, otherworldly landscape. It's why she had placed herself out of her comfort zone and agreed to the trip in the first place. The city choked her lifeforce and made her want to retreat into herself.

But she didn't want Paul to think she was boring. "Yeah, it's certainly something you don't witness every day," she said.

And thank God for that.

***

Paul wanted to see everything and was excited rather than deterred by the growing clusters of people laughing and drinking beer around barbecues as the day wore on and the sun shone brighter. Vanessa pushed up the sleeves of her light sweater, the same one in which she had shivered earlier, and a trickle of sweat ran between her shoulder blades.

Governed by Google Maps on Paul's phone, the couple made their way to the Basilica of Saint Francis, which Vanessa admired for its architecture if not the hordes of vendors outside its doors hawking everything from cough drops to kitchen knives. But here, farther away from the festival, at least, she could carve out a pocket of air for herself. She could breathe, even though the pounding drums—heard but not seen—reverberated outward, through the pavement and up into her bones. Through it all, she kept moving, a phony smile on her face for Paul when he remembered to check if she was still following. And she was; she locked her eyes onto his black tee shirt and tailed him, running at times to keep up.

Smog and grime clogged Vanessa's pores, and the savory, meaty odors of various foods weaved themselves into her thick, curly hair. She watched droplets of liquid spurt out of a large slab of raw, unidentifiable meat as a woman whacked it with a cleaver. Hot bile rushed up her throat in response, but she choked it down, praying the revulsion and dizziness would dissipate.

Everything's fine. You are fine, she told herself, willing it to be true.

"You ready to head back to the hotel?" Paul finally asked, huddled next to a building and out of the crowd, stopping to hydrate from a tepid water bottle bought off a vendor.

"Yes!" Vanessa smiled genuinely this time, thrilled she didn't have to be the one to beg to exit the pandemonium of walking through the streets.

"Alright, let me put the hotel's location in." He fiddled with his phone. "Wow, I didn't realize how close we are! Only a mile away. About twenty minutes."

Vanessa exhaled the tight breath she'd been holding in. She could do this. They were almost there.

***

"Shit," Paul said about fifteen minutes later. "It looks like we can't get through here, either."

They had wandered closer to the melee. The revelers, drunker now, might not have been *trying* to push or shove, but there was nowhere to go but to mill and smush into each other. The multitudes attempted to pass through tapering channels.

"We need to turn around. I think we can try through there." Paul raised his arm to point, almost colliding with another man.

Vanessa sucked in air, hoarding oxygen. The pounding inside her head almost matched the beats of the ever-present drums, blasts of trumpets, and clangs of cymbals. Her ears bled from the continuous assault of shouts and blaring music which had seemed cheerful from the other side of the television screen.

"This way," Paul persisted, reaching to grab Vanessa's shoulder and force her through a narrow passage between a blockade and the back of some tents. Her face and mouth pressed up against the canvas as she tried to evade a new onslaught of bodies, all intent on squeezing past. Some were dancers—a woman's wide, flowing skirt brushed into Vanessa's legs as the boxy cardboard headdress of a man grazed her temple. She hoped her cheap sunglasses would protect her eyes from an unwitting poke or prod as she focused on keeping sight of Paul.

"Babe, my phone's out of juice! I need yours." Paul flattened himself against a tent and reached out to grab Vanessa's. She waited, heart in her throat as the figures clambered past her, almost through her, as Paul input the address. "We need to go this way! We can't get through over here!"

"We just *came* from that way," Vanessa muttered, her voice drowned out by the thundering clamor. Unknowingly, while they had struggled to view the parade earlier, they had advanced closer and closer, now almost in the midst of it as they attempted to find their way. Vanessa focused her eyes on the retreating black speck of Paul's shirt amongst the sea of colorful costumes. More and more people had gotten between them, jammed together like gears in a watch, and Paul wasn't looking behind. Vanessa tried to close the gap, but there was no space; she could only advance one click at a time. Her pulse raced under her skin, faster than the beating drums.

A waft of cigarette smoke blew into her face, and Vanessa squeezed her eyes shut while coughing, harsh and bronchial. Though she halted her own forward motion, the crowd surged on, carrying her. By the time she opened her eyes, she could no longer see her boyfriend.

"Paul!" she yelled, but her voice was devoured by the cacophony amongst her.

She was alone in the crowd.

***

Vanessa swallowed painfully, her water bottle long since empty, the sun setting. She stumbled on, having no other choice. She couldn't break away and had no idea how much time had passed, though her arms and legs burned from exertion, from the effort it took to keep moving. She was in it now, part of the parade.

She wondered idly if Paul had made it back to the hotel or if he, too, were stuck somewhere else in the city. Was he looking for her? Did it even *matter*?

Thinking back to her life in Pennsylvania, Vanessa wished she was there, back in her ho-hum existence working at the university library, a place where she could exist in solitude and quiet, where the days passed by, dull and predictable. Where everyone spoke in whispers and books—not people—surrounded her. How she longed for the mundane rather than the fascinating! She could scarcely believe she was here, in this distant part of the world, away from everything she knew. It didn't seem real.

Yet, here she was, a woman alone in the mass of a writhing, squirming swarm.

With heavy, burning eyes, she glanced at the costumed merrymakers surrounding her, attempting to ground herself in reality. A dragon, perhaps, and a troll? Having nothing better to do, she let her vision embrace the craftsmanship of their regalia: the vibrant colors, the ornate faces.

The sun dropped below the horizon, and Vanessa continued on, all hope of retiring to her hotel now gone. She was alone with no phone and no idea where she was.

Darkness descended, and a sharp, guttural growl emanated from next to her. In the fading light, the costumes took on more fearsome properties. The dragon's sleeves morphed into scales in front of her blurring vision. The troll's vacuous, papier mâché eyes lit up and sparkled as they turned to her, drinking her in.

She tried to rub her eyes to clear them, to set things right. But she couldn't move her arms, held tight now by her companions. Vanessa perceived cold pressure as the dragon's teeth clamped into the flesh of her arm while the troll on her other side bit into her yielding neck. A hot gush of blood spilled out of Vanessa's veins.

And they marched on.

SKIN DEEP

Jean paused as she approached the breakroom door, clearing her throat. She knew they were talking about her. They always did, but she'd be damned if she'd let them see how it bothered her. Sure enough, she heard a peal of laughter followed by a shushing noise, but her coworkers were all smiles when she made her way in.

"Don't you look fetching in your pretty suit today!" Kendall chirped, fluttering her fake eyelashes.

Jean had noticed many of the girls were wearing those these days, but she didn't understand it. It looked like Kendall had stuck a butterfly to each eyelid, or like she might levitate her pert little body into the air if she blinked too hard. Jean didn't bother wearing makeup anymore, but all she'd ever needed back in the day was a coat or two of Maybelline to perk up her eyes.

She barely gave a grunt of acknowledgement, knowing her appearance didn't cut the mustard when it came to today's fashion. Back in her younger days, Jean had enjoyed flipping through *Glamour* magazine and experimenting with fashion trends, but she now preferred comfort and value. Appraising Kendall's choice of outfit, a midriff-baring blouse and short skirt despite the chill of the late spring morning, Jean doubted Kendall appreciated her conservative brown pantsuit. When she got ready that morning, she thought the blue shell she wore underneath brought out her eyes, but now, next to Kendall and the other young people, she felt dowdy and out of touch. "Let me get my coffee, and I'll be out of your way."

"I'd just *die* to have some of that full-fat creamer you're using, and with real sugar, too," Kayla said. "But I need to be bikini-ready for my trip to Cabo next month!"

Jean offered a weak smile and tried to block out the flurry of chatter that followed—something about Kayla thinking her boyfriend might propose, and then a rather heated discussion between Kendall and Ryan about macros and micros, whatever that meant. She simply didn't understand the lives and concerns of these twenty-somethings.

Sitting down in the semi-isolation of her cubicle, Jean gulped her coffee and sighed. She didn't know how much longer she could do this. She'd been with Samson, Green, & Associates for over forty years now, right out of high school, back when the men whose names were on the sign worked there. Though the company had continued to flourish since their retirement, when their entitled offspring took over, Jean longed for the good old days when propriety ruled and women knew to cover themselves in the office. Back when, if you had a tattoo, you had the decency to keep it a secret, not flaunt it like Ryan with his full sleeve on display to all potential clients.

No, she didn't understand this generation, no matter how many hours she slogged away with them. Others in Jean's age group worked at the company, but they were in senior roles, unlike Jean, whose lack of a college degree limited her upward mobility and kept her at an entry-level salary.

At least Jean enjoyed the work, losing herself for hours crunching numbers. She often wore headphones to listen to the soothing sounds of Michael Bolton and Celine Dion rather than hear the non-stop, chipmunk-like chitter of her coworkers, who seemed to spend more time gossiping with each other than completing their work. And yet, Ryan was *her* supervisor based on the piece of parchment he received from some second-rate institution of higher education. Jean's blood boiled when she let herself think about it, and she knew that was bad for her heart, so she tried to remain content with her lot in life, simple as it was.

And it *was* simple. With a salary barely above the poverty level, Jean lived in the same apartment she had rented after moving out of her parents' house. There had been a few men over the years who showed an interest, but none had worked out, and Jean grew weary of putting herself out there, hinging her happiness on a man. She took up knitting and had once prided herself on gifting her coworkers with unique scarves and winter hats at Christmas, but she had stopped when she overheard a former recipient equating her handiwork to that of a kindergartner. Now, she kept her hats and scarves for herself and decorated her apartment with her craft, transforming the drab rooms into her own safe haven, a place where she could enjoy her own company.

Although their official workday ended at five o'clock, she noticed Ryan and the girls heading for the door at half-past four. Jean graced them all with a dour, meaningful glare for their early departure.

Kayla waggled her long, talon-like fingernails at her. "Toodles. Gotta get our table for trivia at the bar. We'd ask you, but..." she pouted, letting the sentence hang in the air.

Ryan was unapologetic. "Don't forget to lock up, and I also want that inventory report emailed to me tonight so I can place an order next week." Unsmiling, he raised his hand in what Jean thought was a wave, but it turned out he was smoothing back his manscaped eyebrows.

Once they left, Jean breathed a sigh of relief. There were others in the building, most likely, but, alone in the accounts payable office, she could complete her tasks in blessed peace. She stood up, relishing the sensation as she stretched her shoulders, working out the kinks from being hunched over her computer all day. Grabbing her notepad and pen, she made her way to the supply closet.

She could leave the confinement of her cubicle, but she couldn't escape her annoyance at Ryan for relegating this task to her. Sure, he was the supervisor, but Kendall and Kayla were at her level, and she had seniority over them. *Decades* of seniority. What did they have on her? Youth and beauty. And maybe the ability to be fun. Jean had been told many times in life that she wasn't much fun, but she didn't care. Jean would rather be dependable than frivolous.

So *she* got the grunt work while her flirty, scantily-clad coworkers sneaked out early, day after day. Earlier in her career, Jean had adored visiting the supply closet and organizing it. The brightly-colored stacks of folders, orderly boxes of pens, and rows of staplers elicited joy in her soul. Truth be told, the company didn't need all the supplies anymore since so much of their work was computer-based, yet Ryan placed an order every month. Maybe he was selling supplies on the side; how Jean would relish turning him in for betraying the company!

As she counted items and marked her notepad, Jean caught a glimpse of herself in the full-length mirror. An odd addition to a supply closet, she hadn't noticed it before and guessed that Kendall or Kayla had tacked it up to admire their toned physiques and glamorous—though trashy—ensembles. In the harsh fluorescent lighting, the face that glowered back at her might have been that of a troll: droopy, fleshy jowls; puffy, purple bags under the eyes; deep, sharp wrinkles; pale, thin lips. Even her eyes, which she thought to be her best feature, appeared watery and dull. Taking in a deep breath, Jean stepped backward to behold her full self: a frumpy, aging woman in a cheap, ill-fitting suit.

Jean was no Blanche DuBois, full of vanity, but it had been years since she looked at herself in such unforgiving light; what she saw jolted her system.

Picturing the smooth, taut skin of her coworkers, Jean felt a strong pang of jealousy. How lucky to be unencumbered by age and decay. How fortunate to peer in the mirror at oneself and feel pride rather than revulsion.

Glancing at the supply materials in front of her, Jean had an idea. She closed the door of the supply closet and removed her clothes, stripping down to her underpants. *Granny panties*, she imagined her coworkers would say.

She stared at her near-naked body in the mirror and picked up scissors and a roll of duct tape. Sucking in her soft, doughy stomach, she wrapped a piece of the hefty tape around her waist as tightly as she could, then added another and another, until she had a sort of skirt, short and tight like Kendall might wear.

There. Her proportions were more pear-shaped than hourglass, but it was an improvement. She worked from the bottom up: clear, thick tape to lift each sagging breast; whiteout to brighten her coffee-stained teeth and stubby fingernails. When the Scotch tape she used to hold back her jowls failed, she picked up a stapler. Just a little pinch on the right side and left, two times each, and her jawline could cut, if not glass, maybe Styrofoam. Jean wiped away the trickles of blood with a finger, rouging her pale lips and highlighting her cheekbones.

Jean smiled in the mirror. A thinner waist, tighter skin... but the whiteout was wearing off. She painted her teeth with another layer.

But now she didn't like the look of her large, squashed areolas peeking through the clear tape. She reached for the black duct tape to complete her minidress.

Feeling sleepy despite the early hour, Jean tried to open her jaw to yawn, but the staples held too tight. While moving her hand to cover her mouth, since Jean's mother taught that a lady never gapes like a slack-jawed fool, she noticed the wobble of flab on her upper arm. She spotted the paper cutter and went to work.

***

When Fred, the custodian, stopped by the accounts payable office Friday night, making his rounds, he was surprised to find the door unlocked and all the lights on.

"Hello?" he called. Sometimes, the older lady liked to work late, even though he knew for a fact she didn't get overtime.

He was met with silence. Well, she *was* getting up there. Maybe she forgot.

He turned up the music on his earbuds and got back to work, locking up when he left.

***

Ryan didn't check his email until Saturday morning—he was out late clubbing and hadn't really needed that report, anyway. He just hated how the old hag smirked with disapproval at the rest of them, so, as her supervisor, it was his duty to ride her a bit and put her in her place. He had to admit that she was a conscientious employee, though, so he was shocked not to find her email. But it was self-care Saturday, and he needed his rest, so he put it out of mind.

Ryan was the first one to the office on Monday morning, which was odd. Maybe Jean was trying to prove some sort of point—first, by failing to send him the report, and now, by not beating him to work as she regularly did.

Something felt off. And was that her purse sticking out from underneath her desk?

"Jean? Are you here?" Maybe she was playing some sort of trick to get back at him for sticking her with the inventory job.

Ryan checked the time. Nine a.m., their official start time, so he didn't expect the girls to show up for a while. And now Jean was officially late. He sighed, annoyed by the tardiness of his underlings. If Jean was AWOL, then *he'd* have to do the inventory himself.

He grabbed a pen and notepad and headed to the supply closet.

SUMMER

FROM THE SEA TO THE SEA

Basking under the rays of the hot Mediterranean sun, Marina stretched out her browning arm and sighed in contentment. She couldn't stop admiring the new, diamond-encrusted band on her finger joining the much bigger glittering rock. If only her mother could see her now, toned and taut in a bikini on the pristine pink sand, a glamorous married woman. How her mother would seethe and rage with jealousy.

But Marina's mother wouldn't ever see her daughter living it up with her new husband at the swanky all-inclusive resort. Marina had seen to that.

***

Frank returned a few minutes later, tropical drinks sweating in his hands. "There was a line at the bar. Some entitled prick insisted on Grey Goose, and the bartender had to run inside for it." His handsome brow furrowed at the retelling.

Marina thought that Frank could act pretty entitled himself, insisting on changing rooms when they arrived due to the whine of the air conditioner when that's just what air conditioners sounded like, but she nodded in sympathy. "Thanks for this," she said, taking a dainty sip and closing her eyes at the rush of sweetness. It was a slippery slope between acting fun and drinking cocktails while maintaining her hard-won figure. She estimated that she could consume this one indulgence and maybe a vodka tonic during the day and remain within her calorie limit as long as she stuck to a dry salad for dinner. Frank said he liked seeing her eat heartily, but he also hadn't known her as a teenager, back when her mother disciplined her if ever she strayed from a restrictive diet. Back when her thighs chafed together on a hot day and her belly strained against her jeans, threatening to burst them open.

"You'll never be beautiful, Marina, and you're far from clever. The best you can hope for to get a man is to be thin," her mother always said, as if getting a man was the only goal for which Marina should strive. In spite of her mother's dictum, Marina gorged herself whenever she could, stealing money from her mother's purse and running down the street to the convenience store, where she'd load up on pints of Ben & Jerry's and potato chips to binge secretly in her room.

How she had hated her mother's punishments after being caught. Her mother installed a lock on the outside door of her room in their small apartment, and Marina would survive for days on nothing but tepid diet ginger ale and saltine crackers, forced to use a cut-open gallon jug as a toilet.

When she disobeyed, her mother wouldn't even allow her to go to school, so Marina fell further and further behind in her studies. She barely graduated from high school for all the days she missed, but her mother had won: Marina was thin.

But angry.

***

As they lay listening to the crash of waves, Frank stroked Marina's arm. "I was thinking you could wear that red dress to dinner tonight."

Marina knew he wanted to strut her around, a piece of arm candy, letting all the other men in the resort ogle her and envy him. She suspected Frank married her for what he believed she represented: youth, beauty, and privilege. He didn't know how hard she worked to project these qualities, from lying about her age and background to how much time she spent on her beauty routine. He was pushing forty, and she was only twenty-eight, but her forged driver's license claimed twenty-three. The story that her parents died in a car accident after she graduated high school was far more palatable than the truth, that she left her mother in a bathtub in rural Pennsylvania, half a bottle of prescription pills crushed into her wine glass, before fleeing to California.

Her mother got it wrong—Marina *was* clever, after all.

***

Later, long after they'd lain down in the mahogany four-poster bed for the night, Marina awoke in darkness. They'd left a window open rather than use the AC, and the cool breeze fluttered the gossamer curtains. Frank, glutted with Ouzo and rich food, snored away, but Marina ate little that night, her tight dress allowing only bird-like portions. But Frank had dug in heavily, sweating away, tearing into the souvlaki and moussaka with a vigor that matched the way he ripped off her dress. He'd torn the fabric in his frenzy, but he said he'd buy her another. That's what men like Frank did: destroyed what they believed belonged to them without any thought to their carelessness.

Marina briefly entertained the idea of leaving Frank in a bathtub, all that booze and a handful of Oxys in his system. Frank knew he shouldn't mix, but he complained often about his old football injury and wasn't always careful when self-medicating. If she just helped nature take its course… but he didn't deserve that, not like her mother had.

She pressed her eyelids shut, willing sleep to return, to wake up to another relaxing day on the beach with little to do other than look good for her husband. This is what she wanted, wasn't it? She had triumphed; she had reeled in her big fish, and now she could reap the fruits of her labor.

But she couldn't shut her mother's voice out of her head, the years of criticisms.

Marina.

She sat up, her eyes popping open. That voice wasn't in her head; it seemed to be coming from outside.

But it couldn't be. She was on her honeymoon, and her mother's voice had been stilled long, long ago.

Marina.

Louder now, more insistent. Marina knew what happened when she kept her mother waiting.

Silently, she crept to the bathroom, pulled on the lush hotel robe over her silk nightgown, and opened the sliding glass door.

Marina, I'm warning you. Come now.

She stepped onto the sand, cool now under her bare feet, and looked around for the source of the noise. Maybe it was a prank somehow. But who would prank her? Who even *knew* her former life? All that remained were awful memories and her first name. She liked her name, the one blessing her mother had bestowed amongst everything else.

The stars glittered in the blackened sky, crisper and brighter than they did back home. Marina glanced behind and saw she had traversed the sand maybe thirty yards from her hotel room, yet she had hardly noticed that she kept walking, searching for the source of that beckoning call.

Come to me.

How many times she had heard her mother's demands over the years, and how many times she had been forced to answer, until that one final night. Her mother enjoyed a relaxing bath, and Marina had made it an eternal one, no longer able to cope with the abuse.

She'd never looked back—never googled the aftermath, just paid the man she met through a coworker for her new identity and moved on. In the years since she'd left, she worked every job she could find and squirreled away the money she made, living in cramped apartments with several roommates; saving up to afford the breast implants, hair extensions, lip fillers, skin treatments, and designer clothing; and transitioning to a glossy version of her former self, one who could catch a rich husband.

A jot of ice hit her as a wave lapped her ankles; lost in thought, Marina had wandered to the coastline. She walked a step closer, up to her toned calf muscles, to see what she could stand, to feel the power and wrath of the sea, and that's when frigid fingers clasped onto her ankles, pulling her farther from shore.

Come back to me. Her mother's voice permeated the air around her, seeming to come from all sides, as water filled her mouth. She kicked her legs, trying to right herself, only to be slammed back down by another crushing wave before she could raise her head to gasp for air.

No longer turquoise and charming, the inky sea closed over her. She couldn't scream, cry for help, or breathe; Marina inhaled salt water through her mouth and nose every time she tried. Despite her rigid exercise regime, her muscles couldn't overpower the fury of the churning waves.

Her face smashed repeatedly into rocks and shards of shells on the seabed, scraping and chafing her skin. Marina tasted blood in her mouth along with other sour, familiar flavors, ones she hadn't tasted since Pennsylvania: diet ginger ale and saltines.

Her dead mother was here somehow, exacting her revenge. Marina inhaled more and more saltwater, her lungs burning and her stomach filling as she prayed for a savior who would never arrive. When she killed her mother, she sealed her own fate.

Marina's heart slowed and stopped, and the blackness of the water enveloped her last shreds of consciousness. Her final thoughts were of her mother and the mistakes they both made.

One night long ago, satiated on wine and flush with money after a successful insurance scam, her mother had stroked Marina's hair tenderly, the only time Marina remembered a soft touch. "Your name means 'from the sea,'" she told her.

And to the sea Marina returned, her bloated, decomposing body washed up and discovered weeks later by local children under the blazing sun.

(IN)TERMINA(B)L(E)

Suitcase in hand, Jackson checked his watch and suppressed a sigh. With only two check-in desks open and the inevitable customer service troubles, the line hadn't budged in the last ten minutes. He'd overheard the raised, heated voices of the British couple as they debated with the airline passenger service assistant as the line snaked longer. The bulging stomach of the man behind him began to press into his elbow.

If the pace didn't pick up soon, Jackson might not make it through security in time. And if he missed his first flight, from Philly to Chicago O'Hare, it could jeopardize the entire trip. It was a close call as it was, with merely an hour at O'Hare before his connection to LAX. If he didn't make it there tonight, he'd miss tomorrow morning's meeting, and that was *not* a viable option.

As project manager of the upcoming technology release at the investment bank, Jackson needed to meet with the coders to ensure they delivered a quality product to the risk management team. Since most of them were remote workers dispersed throughout the country, they'd interacted strictly on conference and Zoom calls for the past couple of months. To ensure the biggest release of the year went smoothly, Jackson's boss, Reggie, insisted they all come together. "Face time is good time," he had said before griping about the cost of flying Jackson business class.

Hell, Jackson deserved to fly in style on the company's dime. And if Mallory, the VP of risk management operations, looked as hot in the flesh as she did on Zoom, the trip would be worth it in more ways than one.

If he made the flight, that is. Although he'd left with plenty of time to spare, the construction on I-476 placed a huge monkey wrench into his plans. His voice hoarse from swearing at other drivers from the confines of his car, Jackson made it to the airport a full hour later than he had hoped.

Finally, the line lurched forward. The British couple continued to bicker away, but the family of five at the other desk had moved on, boarding passes in hand. But that still left about twenty people ahead of him.

I should've listened to Katie, Jackson thought, aggravated that his soon-to-be ex-wife had been right. With the increased travel he was doing for work, she had suggested registering for TSA Pre-Check. He'd sprung for the $78 fee, but it seemed impossible to get an appointment that worked with his demanding schedule, not to mention the additional three hours of driving to and from Philly. There wasn't enough time. If he even got through this line, he'd wait like a schmuck at security.

Jackson didn't have time for a lot of things. When Katie had taken the job of Director of Student Success at Blackthorn University, necessitating the family's move to rural Pennsylvania, Jackson had begrudgingly agreed; after all, he could work remotely. But he missed the hustle and bustle of the city, and now he had to work harder to keep his name at the forefront of the boss's mind. Jackson felt like Katie owed him for messing up his lifestyle. If she nagged at him to do something, he wouldn't say no, but nor would he do it. If he waited long enough, she'd complete the grocery shopping, cooking, cleaning, and most of the childrearing herself while he texted his friends and messed around on the internet. Katie had a full-time job with her own expectations at work, but *some*one needed to handle such things, and it wasn't going to be him. He'd made his sacrifice.

If more efficient, perhaps Jackson would have had more time for such home responsibilities. As it was, he drove into town and parked near the university almost every day with his laptop to sit at Starbucks and work, but he wasted quite a bit of time ogling the college girls in their tight little tops jiggling their tight little asses. He knew he'd never bump into Katie, who worked through lunch every day, eating a packed sandwich at her desk so she could meet their six-year-old daughter, Fiona, at the bus stop. He wasn't worried about running into her co-workers, either, since he had no idea who the hell they were. Katie had been invited to some gatherings with them, but he had discouraged it, saying that he couldn't socialize with anyone from work living all the way out here, so it wasn't really fair if *she* got to.

And then there was his workout schedule cutting into his free time—he liked to keep himself in peak physical condition, which Katie should have appreciated more when she had the chance. She'd let herself go ever since Fiona was born, not even using the gift certificate he'd gotten her for the gym last year for Mother's Day.

Waiting in that line, with nothing else to do, the events of the last year projected like a mental photo montage: the big fight after he didn't show up at Fiona's school's open house, the expression on Katie's face when he called her an unhealthy role model when she brought home Burger King instead of cooking dinner. What was the straw that broke the camel's back when it came to Katie leaving him, taking their daughter and moving to a small apartment across town? Maybe Jackson would've found out if he had agreed to couples therapy, but he didn't have time for that, either.

Jackson's heart rate began to climb. As the minutes ticked away, unpleasant sensations assaulted him: the acrid stench of body odor from one or more of his line companions; intermittent squawks and loud, garbled voices on the intercom system; the pressure of this man's thinly clad flesh against his arm. He closed his eyes for a moment and took a few deep breaths, willing his anxiety to lower, praying that this would all be hurried along.

While Jackson enjoyed discovering new places and wasn't bothered by the plane ride itself, even with the cramped legroom and close proximity to others, he loathed the *process* of travel: the interminable wait and stress, the rushing around just to stand in line, the short tempers of fellow passengers and airport staff. He wished he were past this, sitting at the meeting in the conference room where he could shine, working the room and establishing protocols, schmoozing and making everyone feel special even though he couldn't have cared less about them as individuals—these people simply needed to perform their functions. But fragile egos required management, so he played the game, smiling away, letting his baby blues work their magic. If things went well with the release, he might be on the fast track to a promotion to managing director of the projects team.

Jackson pulled out his phone and tried to distract himself with social media, but he didn't give a shit about the hippy-dippy music festival his sister attended with her loser boyfriend or any of the other inane content his family, friends, and coworkers were sharing; what he *wanted* was his boarding pass. He idly checked Katie's Instagram to see what she and Fiona were up to, but she hadn't posted anything. It was what, Tuesday? The most exciting thing Katie would have going on was maybe a phone call with her mom.

He tried to review his talking points for the meeting, but he couldn't concentrate. Removing his tie and stowing it in his messenger bag, he undid the top button of his shirt. Despite the moderate air conditioning inside, the June heat had wilted him on the brief walk from the shuttle to the terminal, and his armpits bloomed with a dampness that had yet to dissipate. There was no need for him to be dressed like this since the meeting wasn't until tomorrow, but he wanted to look professional when arriving at the hotel in case he ran into anyone important, mainly Mallory. He'd gotten his hair and beard trimmed to look sharp, and he knew he cut an impressive figure with his jacked physique in his slim fit suit. As he noticed other guys around his age appearing comfortable in tee shirts and cargo shorts, though, he wondered if he'd overdone it.

He barely made eye contact with the paunchy, middle-aged woman at the desk, but she wasn't winning any awards with her communication skills, either. She didn't even bother to smile, not that it would likely improve her looks any. Jackson passed over his booking confirmation and ID, then loaded his suitcase onto the conveyor belt, only receiving a curt nod from the woman as she handed him his boarding pass.

Not that he really cared; friendly banter would waste time. Rounding the corner, he stifled a groan as he eyeballed another long line. Though he wouldn't need to remove his shoes, suit jacket, or laptop for some time, Jackson took a moment to glance at his boarding pass to check for his gate, and that's when he saw it: Instead of Groups 1 or 2, standard on several airlines for business class, it said Group 6. That couldn't be right.

Jackson gritted his teeth together, feeling his skin flush with rage, wishing he could have a sip of water, or, better yet, a shot of tequila to take the edge off. He couldn't do anything about this now; no way was he losing his place in this line let alone going back to the other one. Maybe he could talk to them at the gate and rectify the problem. He—well, the bank—had paid good money for business class, and he was damn sure going to get his rightful seat on the plane.

If he made it. *If* there was time.

Shifting his weight from left to right, strumming his fingers on the strap of his carry-on, and blowing hot air through his nostrils, Jackson waited, his rage building. Inching closer to the conveyor belt, he readied himself to pounce on a bin to ensure a quick passage.

But the old woman in front of him had liquids in her bag, and she spread her belongings all over the place, blocking him. Jackson took a deep breath, lifted the woman's bag out of the way, grabbed a bin, and pushed past her to the walk-through metal detector.

It beeped. Of course it did.

"Sir, please step to the side," the TSA agent commanded.

Jackson's left eye twitched in frustration as the agent slowly moved the wand over his body and patted him down before ultimately waving him through.

Thrusting his feet into his shoes, grateful he'd opted for loafers, Jackson stuffed everything else into his bag, not bothering to affix his belt or replace his suit jacket. He peeked at his watch, fearful of what it would tell him, his panic mounting.

Twenty minutes until takeoff. He might just make it.

Adrenaline coursed through Jackson's veins as he began sprinting toward his gate, dodging baby strollers and leisurely walkers. Sweat flowing from his pores, he searched for the elusive A-13 sign.

Jackson struggled on as a wave of exhaustion overtook him. Shouldn't he have reached his gate by now? Something wasn't right here—this wasn't how he remembered the setup of the Philadelphia International Airport, and he'd been here a hundred times. He plodded on.

How long had he been running? He slowed to a shuffle, no longer remembering the gate number or where he was trying to go.

What was he doing at an airport, anyway? How had he gotten here? Where was he going?

His mind clouded with confusion.

***

Suitcase in hand, Jackson checked his watch and suppressed a sigh. With only two check-in desks open and the inevitable customer service troubles, the line hadn't budged in the last ten minutes.

***

In his back yard, at home, Jackson's corpse lay crushed under two fallen branches of an enormous pine tree, his fingers still clasped around a bottle of Troeg's Perpetual IPA. His head had smashed like a watermelon, spilling brain matter and blood like seeds and juice on and around the Adirondack chair. His ribcage had broken, his organs obliterated.

He had heard the first loud crack of warning as the heavier branch descended, briefly suspended by another limb, but he'd been thinking about his upcoming trip to L.A. and what his future might hold. He didn't make the connection to what caused the sound until the second fracture, about ten feet above, so he didn't have time to get up before the combined weight of the heavy wood plummeted down.

No, Jackson never had time. Before the split, Katie had asked him to call the tree guy to check that it was safe, but he'd never gotten around to it.

But now, as Jackson's soul flitted about an airport in another realm, he had all eternity at his disposal. His transgressions on earth weren't heinous enough to send him to the innermost layers of hell, so there would be no flaying of skin or removing of fingernails, but perhaps his punishment was close: He would wait in line, check in to his flight, and go through airport security for perpetuity.

A GIFT FOR AVERY

I was never fond of the thing, even though it caught my eye from the moment I saw it—*her*. Walking through Blackthorn Antiques, I almost passed right by; a woman who prefers new rather than used items, I only entered the establishment on a whim to find a birthday gift for my difficult-to-please mother.

But, while searching for the elusive 1950s bakeware which my mother adores, I stumbled upon a doll unlike any I could buy at Target. With its hand-painted porcelain skin, realistic acrylic eyes, and goldenrod dress, it almost looked like a miniature child ready for a party. "Hi! My name is Linda. I am like a real girl. I want to be your friend," the tag attached to the doll read. Unlike most of the stained and worn merchandise in the store, Linda remained sealed and pristine in her box, a relic from another era.

Linda even had her own little doll, Cathy, attired in a matching dress. I smiled at the now old-fashioned names, so different than the Kendalls and Maddies of today.

Something about this odd doll spoke to me, but *only* as Avery's mother. It would never have appealed to me during childhood, as I always preferred Barbies, reveling in the beautiful dresses and tiny plastic shoes, thinking how marvelous it would be to dress like that when I grew up. My daughter, however, was another story: She was *obsessed* with dolls, especially realistic ones, looking to them, perhaps, as friends to help fill the void left by her father's absence.

Yes, this doll was perfect for my Avery. It was easy to understand why she became so desperate for affection. Although her father, Jeff, a functional alcoholic, fought me in court for visitation, he was always "working on a case" when he was supposed to pick his daughter up from daycare or take her for the weekend. While he was, indeed, a workaholic, one of a long string of problems which acted as a catalyst to the dissolution of our marriage, I knew him well enough to decipher that "working on a case" was sometimes code for a date with a bottle of Jack Daniels. As a lawyer myself, becoming a single mom was no easy transition. Still, my daughter came first, and it fell on me to pick up the pieces of our lives.

"Your credit card, ma'am?" the clerk asked, bringing me back to the present. I paid and left, hiding my purchase in the trunk, to pick up Avery from the daycare center.

After strapping her into her child seat, I told Avery about the surprise. Her eyes lit up.

"Did you get her? Did you get my doll?" Her voice seldomly expressed such excitement since the divorce. With all of the recent stress Avery had endured, I had told her days earlier that she wouldn't need to wait for her actual birthday to receive her gift.

"Hold your horses. Let's get home first to see," I said, not wanting errant pieces of cardboard and twist ties all over the car. I eased into traffic, taking a quick peek in the rearview mirror to feast upon the obvious joy in her eyes.

Avery flew into the house bubbling with anticipation. "Now, Mommy? Can I see her *now*?"

Making a big show of it, I hid the parcel behind me, finally brandishing it in front of Avery. "Ta-da!" So much for wrapping paper; I would get her something little and wrap it for her to open on her actual birthday.

Her face radiated delight. "Oh, wow! Thank you, Mommy! Thank you so much!" No sooner had I helped Avery release Linda and Cathy from the box than she ran to her room to "introduce" them to her other dolls.

***

At about six the next morning, I awoke panicked from a deep sleep after hearing soft sobs emanating from Avery's room. I assessed the problem from her doorway: On the floor, shattered, lay a porcelain doll, an expensive, raven-haired beauty that had been Avery's favorite, a splurge I had purchased at a conference to assuage my guilt for leaving my child.

"Look, Mommy," she cried, pointing to the jagged pieces of the doll's remains. As if reading my thoughts, Avery said, "I didn't do it, Mommy, I promise. She was lying there when I woke up. Cyril must have knocked her off my dresser!" Our orange tabby cat was a lovable troublemaker with a penchant for pulling out push pins from bulletin boards with his teeth, stealing food right off of our plates, and pawing objects off shelves. "I'll miss Angelica *so* much. Naughty Cyril!" Her normally placid face twisted in anger.

"I know, honey." I sighed, wondering how I could help my unlucky daughter get over yet another disappointment, as the doll was beyond repair. "Maybe I can get you a replacement someday." I started cleaning up the carnage, as much to remove the horror from Avery's eyes as to protect her delicate feet from cuts.

"It's okay, Mommy," Avery said, suddenly calm, drying her tears with her nightgown. "I don't need another Angelica. Now Linda is my favorite doll." She hugged her prized possession closer against her chest, and I felt a surge of relief that my choice had been such a hit.

Later that morning, I made a shocking discovery. The latch on the cat door was fastened; Cyril had been locked out of the house since after his dinner the evening before. He couldn't have gotten into Avery's room and knocked the doll off the shelf.

Avery probably broke it on accident and didn't want to confess, I rationalized, a little hurt that she lied to me, but that's what kids do. *Or maybe the doll was balanced precariously, and gravity took its course.*

The morning after that was far worse; I jolted awake to Avery's screams.

Cyril lay at the foot of Avery's bed, limp. Although he often slept curled up with her, it was obvious that he wasn't sleeping this time. He simply looked *off*, a lump rather than my beloved companion.

"He was an old cat," I told Avery as soon as I composed myself. "This is so, so sad, but at least now Cyril doesn't have to live with any pain."

But none of this was true. Eight was middle-aged for a cat, not old, and Cyril had received a clean bill of health from the vet the month before. I held Avery tightly and we cried together, mourning the loss of our sweet boy.

In the privacy of my own room, I examined Cyril's stiffening body, wincing as I touched his motionless form. His glossy fur was already starting to dull and his sightless, cloudy eyes protruded. Poor, poor guy.

Then I noticed his collar; it was pulled far too tight! I normally kept the prong in the fourth or fifth hole, but it was in the tightest setting. Had he strangled to death? Weeping harder, knowing it was already too late, I loosened what had served as Cyril's death noose.

A tiny scrap of goldenrod fabric fluttered to the ground.

Linda. The *doll*. Goosebumps arose on my bare arms.

"Get a grip," I said aloud. "Dolls can't kill cats." I felt stupid and childish.

Nevertheless, as soon as I heard Avery close the door to use the bathroom, I sneaked into her bedroom. There lay Linda on the center of the bed, the place of honor.

I approached slowly, paranoid despite every rational fiber of my being insisting that there was *no way* that my suspicions could be true. Linda and Cyril had both been on the bed, and Avery had touched each of them, so it wasn't impossible for a small piece of fabric to end up on the cat. Tentatively, I picked it up—picked *her* up. The large, flat eyes seemed to be watching me, judging me.

Cats shed when frightened, and Cyril's orange hair covered Linda's dress and hands. That's what got me: the hands. I knew then what those tiny, inanimate fingers had done, as crazy as it sounded. Terrified, I started to run out of the room when I tripped. I looked down at my feet and saw the cloth corpse of Linda's doll, Cathy, torn to shreds.

As calmly as I could, I got ready for the day, knowing I'd need to make a stop at the animal hospital to set up cremation for unfortunate Cyril. I'd need a story, too, for how could I tell the truth about what had happened? Instead, I'd claim I had found him with his collar caught on something, a rational explanation for his death. It was all too much.

While Avery ate her Cheerios downstairs, I locked her door from the outside. I wasn't taking any chances with that abhorrent *thing*. I'd have to figure something out, though, and do so fast. I didn't think Avery was in any real danger. Then again, I hadn't thought Cyril was, either.

In the car on the way to daycare, I forced a note of cheer into my voice as I brought up disposing of the doll. Out of necessity, more falsehoods spilled from my lips. "How about if I return Linda and get you another doll? I saw this gorgeous doll named Francesca. She's beautiful—*much* better than Linda. But she's really expensive, so I'd have to return Linda to have enough money to spend on—"

"No," Avery cut me off, her voice firm. "She's my *favorite* doll."

I decided to push the doll off the shelf that night while Avery was sleeping; so what if I couldn't blame it on Cyril? I would invent yet another lie.

***

That evening, I could barely concentrate on the Disney movie we were watching. Avery had fallen asleep on the couch, snoring, her little chest moving rhythmically up and down. Although she had wanted to run and get Linda as soon as we arrived home that evening, I made excuse after excuse to separate her from her room, away from that horrible *thing*.

Then I heard something, soft at first, unintelligible. I muted the television, even though what I really wanted to do was block out the horror of what I suspected that sound must be.

"Aaaaaaannnnnaaaaaa," the nasal, whining voice called, stretching out the two syllables of my name. Even coming from upstairs, from behind the door of Avery's bedroom, I could hear her. A shiver crept down my back.

"Anna!" The voice summoned me again, more forceful now, and I knew it must be stopped at all costs.

I glanced at Avery, innocent and oblivious on the couch. Gingerly, so as not to wake her, I rose and skulked into the kitchen, heading straight to the butcher block on the counter and grabbing my biggest knife.

Non-weapon-wielding hand leaning on the banister, I tiptoed up the stairs, closing in on the disembodied, demonic voice.

"What will it be like without your daughter, Anna?" Linda paused, her mocking voice sing-song. "Well? You've already lost your husband, and even your cat."

Unlocking the door to Avery's room, holding my breath, I readied myself for attack. At first, I didn't see her; my visage only embraced a litter of doll carcasses, torn apart like carrion, and Avery's framed photograph. Now hanging crookedly from the wall, the glass had been smashed, Avery's beautiful face ripped down the middle.

Then I saw Linda. She was standing—*standing*, on her own two porcelain feet—across the room from me. Her head swung around, owllike. As painted lips curled into a grin, her cold, inhuman eyes locked on mine.

I threw my butcher knife at her.

"Nyah nyah nyah NYAH nyah! You missed me, bitch!" Linda screeched, leaping across the room towards me. Though I tried to run, her tiny hands grabbed my ankle and yanked me back. I flopped to the floor with a thud, surely bruising my body, but that ache was nothing compared to what she did next.

She started chewing into my calf with razor sharp teeth. I flailed my leg, attempting to shake her off to quell the piercing, crippling pain. That thing was *mangling* my flesh.

Growing light-headed from blood loss, I shrieked in agony. My knife was across the room; I had no weapon with which to defend myself and no one to save me from this creature. But if I succumbed to this beast, who would stop her from hurting Avery? I needed to save myself to protect my child.

Contorting my body, I took both fists, one on each side, and punched the distracted, chomping doll's head with as much strength as I could muster. I felt the porcelain give way and shatter, lacerating my hands, as my fists crunched together.

Linda stopped biting. She ceased to *be*, and I lay there bleeding with what appeared to be merely another broken doll. I cried in relief as those inhuman jaws finally stilled.

It was over. I grabbed a shirt from Avery's nearby hamper to wrap around my leg and staunch the bleeding.

Avery entered the room, tears streaking her face. "I saw what happened," she said. Then she glanced at my injured leg. "We'll call 911. We'll say you were attacked by a wild animal outside."

Poor Avery. Not quite five years old, she knew when she needed to lie, just like her mother.

But before I could call for medical attention, despite how much I needed it, we had more pressing business. Since I couldn't walk, I sent Avery to the basement for the sledgehammer.

We crushed the pieces of the monster to shards. Dragging myself to the fireplace, I threw in Linda's remains. I set the fire and watched until everything burned. Only then did I call for help.

I stayed at the hospital for two days, during which time Jeff actually took off work to take care of his daughter. Avery and I agreed that we could never tell him, the doctors, or anyone else what happened; we stuck to the story we had crafted despite how implausible it sounded. How could we tell the truth? It was even *less* believable than the flimsy fiction we had created. I suffered through unneeded rounds of rabies shots to avoid being sent to the psych ward.

Weeks later, on a humid summer morning when I had healed enough to walk with the aid of a crutch, I took Avery to a picnic spot we frequented, a state park near a lake. After my return from the hospital, not wanting to take any chances, we collected the ashes from the fire and sealed them in a plastic bag we had temporarily buried in the back yard. I didn't want that *thing* polluting our ground, so we weighed the bag of ashes down with a couple pounds of rocks and dropped it into the depths of the water to ensure our safety.

I'm not a litterer by nature, but this was the closest I could get to sending that thing back to hell.

We adopted a kitten soon afterward, a gray ragamuffin from a local shelter. Maybe it was too soon after everything that happened, but we needed love. We needed hope. And he will *never* wear a collar.

Avery has endured far more than a girl her age ever should. While I celebrate our survival, I regret the loss of her innocence. With that forfeiture, though, she has gained wisdom, an eerie understanding of the evil that exists in the world.

She *will* survive, even if fractured. She will love, suffer, and experience the triumphs and sorrows of the great and terrible human experience.

And she will never, ever go near a doll again, not even the one her dad got her for her birthday. It's still in the box, packed away in a corner of the basement with the few remaining dolls Linda hadn't destroyed.

I'm sure it will be fine.

ITCH

Colby awoke to discomfort and found his hand curled into a claw, scratching his thigh.

Damn mosquitos. As a landscaper, the summer months wreaked havoc on his flesh despite his daily coatings of bug spray on both his bare skin and clothes. Even in scorching weather, he wore jeans for protection. And *still* those bastards had gotten him.

There were mosquito bites, and then there were *mosquito* bites. This seemed to be the second type. Colby had rubbed himself raw and bloody enough times to know that he needed to resist the urge. Besides, he needed sleep. With another long day in the sun tomorrow, he did *not* want to end up as the guy who snoozed on the job and mowed off his toes.

He lay on his back, hands on his chest over the thin sheet, corpselike, and closed his eyes, listening to the thrum of his AC unit. He willed sleep to come, striving to keep his thoughts away from the gnawing, burning sensation assaulting him.

Inhale. Exhale. Think peaceful thoughts. Colby tried to imagine himself back at the campsite this past weekend. He and his boys had met up for the first time since they'd graduated high school last year, and it was so damn relaxing hanging out by the campfire and enjoying each other's company as they drank beers and gazed up at the stars, searching for constellations.

But even that happy memory couldn't distract him from the prickling insistence on his thigh. It seemed to get hotter, stronger under his sheet, and his desire to attack himself heightened in equal measure.

Six a.m. would be here before he knew it, and then it was non-stop sun, grass, gasoline, bugs, and sweat, plus a few annoying homeowners either bitching at or flirting with him. It would be another long, grim day followed by a short reprieve before starting it all over again. Running a lawn service business wasn't glamorous, but it sure beat how that Prometheus dude got his guts chewed out every day. (Yes, Mrs. Sanchez, he *was* paying attention during that mythology unit in ninth grade English class.)

"Screw this," Colby said aloud as he hopped out of bed. He'd managed bug bites and even some raging cases of poison ivy before with hydrocortisone cream. He turned on the harsh light in the bathroom, waited a moment as his eyes adjusted, and inched up the hem of his boxers to survey the damage.

Instead of the small, red, raised bump he expected, a swelling the size of an egg with a pinprick opening at its center had erupted on his right thigh.

"What the fuck?" He had just touched it five or ten minutes ago and wasn't expecting this... monstrosity. After a frantic scratch around the skin of the infected area, Colby ventured a tentative graze of the blemish itself. With his fingertip, he pushed, like his mom used to do when she was checking if it was time to take a cake out of the oven.

The lump was not only hot but sore, and he left a whitish mark on the otherwise pink area. He pressed harder and felt something move inside. Despite the shape, it wasn't firm or unyielding but squishy, like the old waterbed he had to sleep on when he visited his grandma's house as a kid. Using both hands, he pushed on each side. Green, gelatinous pus started seeping out.

Colby almost vomited, not just from the revolting sight or lightning-hot pain, but from the smell. As the discharge dribbled down his leg, a sulfurous, rancid odor filled the small, windowless bathroom. The more slime that came out, the more that pinprick-sized fissure stretched, until it was as big as a penny, and then a quarter.

But his skin remained swollen. In fact, it was worsening.

Lightheaded and beginning to feel the fingers of real fear creep down his spine, Colby sat on the cool tile and hung his head, looking away from his throbbing, oozing leg, away from whatever it was leaking out of him. Should he call for an ambulance? He knew that this was a bigger job than hydrocortisone cream could handle.

Holding the counter for support, Colby hauled himself back to his feet. Perhaps he should squeeze some more to reduce the protrusion, as the gunk inside of him was clearly the culprit of his discomfort. There was only so much more there could be, right? And then maybe he could bandage the wound and try to get back to sleep.

When he attempted his technique again, pressing on both sides, it almost felt like something was pushing back at him, ready to explode. Maybe this was the core? Colby had watched some gross-out pimple popping videos on TikTok before, but he was unclear on the terminology.

When a sharp, blackened fingernail wormed its way out of the growing hole in Colby's thigh, followed by the digit itself, Colby lost consciousness and plummeted back to the floor, hitting his head hard as he landed. He would experience no more itch, no more pain.

The expanding pool of blood mingled with the almost neon-colored substance that originated not from a mosquito or Colby's body, but from another realm. A shriveled, gray fist and arm worked through the widening orifice, and then the creature's head crowned, ripping the skin with a low crackle. It slithered out, shoulders, torso, legs, and feet, landing with a wet, sticky plop on the floor, reborn.

More than 200 years ago, when Father O'Neill succeeded in exorcizing the demon from a possessed child, he'd failed to banish the murderous beast back to hell. He had to improvise, casting the wretch into the nearest living, nonhuman thing he could find: a blackberry bramble. Not wanting to risk the safety of the child or any other parishioners, Father O'Neill dug up the plant and relocated it far from the village, in a remote area of untamed Pennsylvanian forest.

But time had transformed those woods into Water's Edge State Park, a popular camping destination. When Colby stumbled upon the unexpected treasure on his camping trip, he foraged blackberries for himself and his friends. He was careful as he removed the fruit, but, having filled his mouth with warm, tangy deliciousness, he didn't notice the thorn piercing his jeans and entering his thigh.

This was all the demon needed—a drop of human blood to escape its prison and regrow. It would not risk staying inside a human; not again. Instead, it would work its way out. It only needed a few days inside a host to bide its time.

After feasting on Colby's ruined body, the demon stretched to its full height and slicked back its wet, tangled hair. It left the apartment, on the hunt for fresh meat.

CRAWL SPACE

"Drop it, Toby. Drop it now." Jared sighed in exasperation at the sight of the limp, furry body clenched in his German Shepherd's mouth. Halfway through cooking the ground turkey for his pasta sauce, he'd taken a quick moment to call the dog inside. Those damned rabbits kept getting through the gaps in the fence and making nests, and Toby couldn't resist a sweet baby bunny snack.

But this was bigger. The mother, perhaps. And she wasn't moving.

Toby held fast to his kill, the head locked in his vice-like jaws. It could be worse. At least he wasn't trying to eat it. Jared turned his back to head for the box of dog biscuits, which he shook twice. He hated to reward Toby right now, but he needed the dog to *let go*. Blood was already dripping onto the beige carpeting, and Jared didn't want a bigger mess.

Toby released the carcass, and it landed with a gentle *plop*. With crimson-smeared teeth, he smiled up at his owner and took his treat.

Knowing he could only distract Toby for a few seconds, Jared reached with a garbage bag to bundle up the poor creature.

That's when he noticed two short, pointy ears instead of long, floppy ones. And an extended tail instead of a cotton ball.

Toby had killed a *cat*. Gingerly, Jared placed his palm on the tawny, slick fur, noticing the punctures to search for signs of life. There was nothing—no shallow breaths, no trace of a heartbeat. The glassy green eyes stared ahead, sightless, and the mouth had frozen in a final hiss. The cat's nine lives were up, and the thin purple collar around its neck indicated that someone would be searching for this animal.

"Toby, what did you *do*?" Jared whispered, ignoring the acrid stench of burning meat emanating from the kitchen. The smoke alarm would go off at any moment, but he had to know whose cat this was. Hopefully, it was far from home, lost for a long time, even though its well-nourished form suggested otherwise. Trembling, trying not to look at the stiffening corpse, he moved the ID tag closer: "Peaches. 15 High Street."

Oh, no. This was the next-door neighbor's cat.

"Toby, go to your crate." Jared's tone left no room for misinterpretation. There would be no bites of ground turkey for Toby tonight. He slunk away while Jared turned off the stove, racking his brain for what to do next.

Jared pictured Cindy, his neighbor and the president of the homeowners' association, with her perfect blonde bob and expensive athleisure wear. A widow in her forties, who, according to rumors, had been married to a wealthy and much older man, Cindy spent her days toning her perfect body with Pilates, posting on social media, hosting boozy book clubs, and sticking her nose into other people's business under the guise of neighborliness.

When Jared moved to Blackthorn a year earlier, shortly after he rescued Toby from a shelter, Cindy turned up on his doorstep with a Bundt cake and a word of warning. "Keep that beast leashed and clean up after him. And don't leave him outside barking, disturbing the peace. We don't want to ruin this wonderful neighborhood, do we?" The plastic smile on her face failed to reach her eyes.

"No," Jared stammered. A computer programmer who worked from home, he wasn't accustomed to implied threats from beautiful women. If Cindy was outside gardening when Jared walked Toby, he'd shake his little plastic bag at her to prove he was following her rules. Cindy's pouty lips and elfin nose would scrunch up in disgust, but Jared didn't want any trouble. He sought to enjoy this calm, quiet neighborhood and sit in the back yard with a beer or three on a warm day. Thank God for the high fence to give him some privacy from Cindy's steadfast gaze.

Jared performed a quick Google search on his iPhone to see what could happen if a dog killed a neighbor's cat. *Lawsuit. Euthanasia.* His course was clear; he could not return poor Peaches to her no-doubt wrathful owner.

Honesty was not the best policy if it meant that Cindy would take him down like a criminal, or even worse, have Toby literally put down. Besides, outdoor cats went missing all the time. Peaches could have been hit by a car.

Jared considered driving the cat to a distant neighborhood and leaving it in the street for someone else to find and hit with their car. No one would ever know Toby's role if Jared did that.

But that was too cruel. Jared's mind flashed back to tenth grade English class when he learned about Achilles dragging Hector's dead body through the streets, and look what happened to *him*.

Jared sat down, cross-legged, his head in his hands as he waited for the answer. He couldn't go to Cindy with the sad little corpse, and he wouldn't disrespect Peaches by abandoning her in the street or a Dumpster. He had placed the dead rabbits in his outdoor trashcan, and he had felt bad enough about that. But Peaches was a pet. Even with a rude busybody for an owner, she deserved a proper burial.

Just a couple of weeks past the longest day of the year, it wouldn't be dark for a few more hours. Perhaps if he waited for the cloak of night to fall, he could bury Peaches in his yard, unseen? But what if Toby dug her up? And what if someone *did* see him? He could never be certain when Cindy was watching, especially if her cat was missing, and if she caught him... he shuddered to think of how this woman could punish him.

Then, an inspiration: the crawl space.

Jared hadn't even known it existed until his pipes froze last winter and the plumber told him he needed access to the unfinished area of the basement behind a sheet of plywood. The stone wall stopped, its edges jagged as if someone hit it with a sledge hammer. Jared had watched as the man slithered his six-foot, lanky frame into the tunnel and crawled on his belly, right on top of the dirt. A barely-concealed portal to the outside world, the seldom-used crawl space could provide a hidden burial ground for Peaches, away from Toby's trusty snout, and no one would ever know.

He waited until nightfall and descended to the basement with a shovel and Peaches wrapped in a towel. He would have preferred a more elegant burial shroud, but it was better than a garbage bag.

"I'm so sorry, Peaches," he whispered. He left her on the floor and hoisted himself up, shovel in outstretched arm, into the opening, imagining the spiders, worms, and centipedes squirming inches from his skin.

It was slow, laborious work. With little space above him, not even enough to sit up, Jared had to finagle the shovel at an awkward angle. Unused to manual labor, the handle soon bit into Jared's flesh, and sweat from his exertion pooled between his shoulder blades. He grunted into the dark, prodding and thrusting the dirt, creating a hole about three feet deep. At last, he wriggled out, picked up the now-rigid burial package, placed it in the grave, and restored the soil.

"Bad dog," Jared said to Toby as he walked by, filthy, on his way to the shower. He was ready to put this all behind him. Let sleeping *cats* lie.

***

Peaches's photo was posted all over town by the next day. Jared saw the first flyer, in full color with "Have you seen me?" and Cindy's name, address, and phone number, taped to the door of Dunkin' when he stopped for coffee. Since he worked from home, he needed a routine to force him out of his house, beneath which Peaches would now spend eternity. A deep shame engulfed Jared as he imagined the flesh rotting off her bones in the earth under his kitchen, the worms feasting upon her.

When he stopped at the Shop Rite that evening, Peaches stared out at him again, green eyes accusing, and later when he scrolled through Facebook. He wasn't friends with Cindy, of course, but he saw her post on the town's page.

"SOMEONE HAS SEEN MY PRECIOUS PEACHES! WHERE IS SHE?!?" Cindy's letters, all caps, screamed at Jared from the page. While some of the comments chided her for providing all of her personal information or explained that outdoor cats go missing all the time, many others were "praying for Peaches's safe return!"

But Peaches would *not* be returning. The best thing that could happen was for Cindy to believe her cat had run away.

On the third day, after his morning walk with Toby, Cindy accosted Jared on his front step. "Have you seen my cat?" She thrust a flyer toward him, but Jared held back.

"Whoa, careful Cindy. Please don't get so close to Toby. You know he's afraid of strangers." Jared pulled Toby, who had lunged at Cindy's intrusion into his personal space. "I've told you this. And no, I haven't seen Peaches."

Cindy narrowed her eyes, her Botoxed forehead unmoving, seeming to focus on all of Jared's insecurities: his receding hairline, crooked nose, and bulbous Adam's apple. "Then how do you know her name if you haven't seen her?"

"I've seen your flyers and your Facebook posts. I'm sorry she's missing, but it's nothing to do with me." *Should he have said that? She wasn't implying that he was involved, was she?* He tried to rearrange his face into a mask of concern.

"Well, keep your eyes open. And keep that mangy dog of yours on a leash," she snarled, even though Toby was well-groomed, his brown and black hair silky smooth beneath the heavy-duty harness.

***

Deep in concentration writing code early that evening, Jared snapped to attention after the third or so sharp rap at his door, punctuated with Toby's incessant barking. *Cindy.*

"Stay," he said, but Toby scrambled to the door with him, his toenails clicking on the hardwood foyer floor.

Jared opened the door just a fraction of an inch. "Yes, Cindy, what is it now?" He couldn't keep the annoyance out of his voice despite his role in this woman's distress.

Cindy pushed the door open, thrusting her cell phone in Jared's face. "There's a hole in your fence! I saw it, and I have a photo. My Peaches must've come into your yard, and your brute of a dog—"

Toby, unused to hostile visitors to his home, charged past Jared and threw himself at the screaming woman, taking a nip at her arm and cutting her tirade short as his teeth pierced her flesh.

Cindy cried out in pain.

Jared slammed the door shut behind her and pinned her to it. He couldn't have anyone finding out about Peaches, or about this. Placing his hand over her mouth, he attempted to quell the grating noise.

"Shush, Cindy! Shut up!" Jared whisper-yelled. When Cindy bit his palm, he pulled it away for a moment. Enraged, he fastened both hands around her neck and squeezed.

Skinny, pale, hunched-over-his-desk-all-day Jared kept his unrelenting grip so long and so tight around Cindy's throat that he cut off her airway. After the blood vessels in her eyes burst, she sagged, limp, toward him.

His anger deflated, replaced with panic. As he stepped to the side, mouth agape, her body fell to the floor like a sack of potatoes.

It took him several minutes to regain his wits.

"Cindy?" Crouching next to her, he shook her shoulder. Then he felt for a pulse.

Nothing.

"Are you okay?" He jostled her harder this time, and her head lolled, bloodshot eyes unblinking. "I didn't mean to hurt you. I just wanted you to stop screaming."

He sat there for a while, thinking back to the many times he had yelled at Toby for uncontrolled behavior. Maybe urges could overtake the body, leaving behind rational thought and propriety. Maybe it couldn't be helped, not really.

Jared exchanged a look with Toby.

And then Toby went to his crate as Jared dragged Cindy's cadaver down to the crawl space, where he dug the hole a little bigger and deeper. He curled her supple form around her cat.

***

When Cindy was finally reported missing several days later by one of her loyal book club devotees, the cops canvassed the neighborhood.

One of the other neighbors, Mrs. Jenkins, told the detectives how Cindy had shared personal information online and all over town. "It wasn't wise," she said on the local news. "All kinds of crazies coulda taken it as a personal invitation. They coulda come right to the house and grabbed her, a good-looking woman like that. She shoulda known better than to tell the world where she lived."

Indeed, wherever Cindy went, she hadn't even taken her purse. Only her cell phone was missing. The last ping came from within 100 yards of her house, but the phone was never recovered, and nor was Cindy's body. "The murderer probably smashed the phone, and now he's off who knows where," Mrs. Jenkins hypothesized to the greedy camera lens. Her word was taken as gospel.

After Cindy's possessions were removed and the house sold, a new family moved in. Jared made sure to act friendly when, on an afternoon walk with Toby, he saw the preteen boy riding his bike.

Knowing he couldn't handle another hostile relationship with neighbors, Jared slapped on a wide smile.

"Hello!" Jared called. "I'm your neighbor."

The boy furrowed his brow, staring at the grinning stranger, but then his gaze alighted on Toby, and the distress fell away. "What a cool dog! Can I pet him?" he asked, dismounting from his Schwinn.

"No, sorry. He's unpredictable." Jared hated throwing Toby under the bus like that, making it sound like he was dangerous, but he couldn't risk a difficult encounter.

The boy froze midstride, and Jared waited for the awkwardness that such an exchange often produced. People didn't understand what it was like to have a dog like Toby, a good boy who sometimes let his instincts take over, and they made snap judgments about Jared's beloved companion. But after what happened with Cindy, Jared could relate to Toby's darkness—he understood it now.

But the boy's face broke into a compassionate smile as he stepped backward. "We had a dog like that, too! I get it. You need to respect that some dogs need space."

"Thank you for understanding," Jared said, beaming. "Welcome to the neighborhood."

***

Later that night, before bed, Jared headed downstairs to the basement. In life, he had rarely made an effort at friendliness with his neighbor, but their relationship had evolved. He enjoyed Cindy's presence in his home now that she could no longer judge him, so he checked in on his charges often, like a proper guardian should. He had an obligation to be hospitable. He also knew she liked to stay informed on the goings-on of the neighborhood, being housebound as she was.

"I met one of the new neighbors today. They're dog people," he said. "Good night, Cindy. Good night, Peaches."

Jared went to bed and slept soundly.

THE MIRROR

Looking around the crowded, stuffy antique store, Jessica sighed. "Mom, this is so boring." She couldn't even sit down anywhere; her mother wouldn't let her in case she might ruin a "priceless treasure."

"Just a few more minutes, honey, I promise," Mrs. Macintosh said without looking at her twelve-year-old daughter. She was too busy surveying every knick-knack, chair, and lamp in the establishment.

"Like I haven't heard that before," Jessica muttered under her breath. Her mom was absolutely obsessed with antiques. It was bad enough that she was always dragging Jessica to every store in the state that sold old stuff, looking for items for her decorating business or their house, but now her mother was actually looking for furnishings for Jessica's *room*! All of her friends had at least gotten to pick out their own furniture, but, no, not Jessica. Her mother said that the house needed to have a "universal decorating theme," or something like that, and that meant she was pushing these nasty ancient furnishings into Jessica's own private space.

She pushed the issue one more time, even though she knew she wouldn't get her way. "Are you *sure* you have to pick out my furniture? No one even goes in my room but me, Mom. Your friends and clients don't need to know if my stuff comes from, like, Ikea or Target."

Her fingers caressing yet another prize, Mrs. Macintosh ignored her daughter once again. "Well? What do you think?"

As irritated as she was, Jessica had to admit that the mirror was beautiful. Large and rectangular, the glass was held in place by an intricately carved, mahogany-stained wooden frame. Jessica peered more closely to see the decorative leaves and flowers. "It's pretty, I guess," she admitted.

Mrs. Macintosh beamed, her professionally-whitened, even teeth almost glowing in the shop's dim lighting. "It's fabulous. And look at the price! This little old guy doesn't have a clue how much his antiques are worth." She lowered her voice conspiratorially, stealing a quick glance in the direction of the stooped, prune-faced man behind the cash register. "I guess he doesn't know the ins and outs of the business."

Jessica rolled her eyes behind her mother's back. She hated how her mom gloated when the owners were more interested in servicing their shoppers than making a quick buck. Rather than respecting their honesty, Mrs. Macintosh seemed to think she was superior to them since she knew how to squeeze every penny out of her clients. Jessica loved her mom, but she didn't understand why she was so greedy.

They walked up to the proprietor of Blackthorn Antiques. Mrs. Macintosh left the mirror where it was, feigning disinterest. "Hello?" she said, though she was right next to him. "I think there might be a mistake? I like your little mirror there, but the price seems awfully high for something that isn't by a known designer. And the condition is only fair, at best."

Jessica tried to block out the back-and-forth haggling between her mom and the little old man. It was so humiliating, hearing her mother speak to this poor soul like he was cheating her instead of the other way around. Finally, it appeared to be over, for Mrs. Macintosh bore a triumphant smile on her face.

"Young lady?" It took Jessica a moment to realize that the old man was addressing her. "Take good care of that mirror," he told her in a scratchy voice. "It has a lot of history."

"Yes, sir," Jessica answered. That was what her mother loved and she hated about antiques. While Mrs. Macintosh adored imagining all of the people who had used the item before, Jessica thought it was kind of gross, like sharing a tissue someone else had blown their nose in. Oh, well; it was just a mirror. All people had done was *look* in it before. No harm there.

Later that night, after much prodding from his wife, Mr. Macintosh hung the mirror in Jessica's room. Jessica had to admit that her mother was a wonderful decorator, for the mirror looked at home amongst her other furniture. Except for the few "modern" possessions she was allowed to display, Jessica's room now looked like it could have come from a century ago with the beautiful wooden four poster bed, dowry chest, and armoire. As much as she would have liked to display posters of her favorite singers and actors, like her other friends did, she knew her room looked magnificent.

Jessica peered into her new mirror, marveling that the glass still looked so fresh and unclouded. Her mother had once told her that mirrors often failed to survive the ages; even if the glass remained unbroken, mirrors could easily scratch or become tarnished. Yet this mirror only revealed her reflection.

Studying her long, straight dark hair and her deep-set, hazel, heavily lashed eyes, Jessica somehow felt prettier reflected in this mirror. Feeling obnoxious and vain, she took one last glimpse of herself and finally peeled her eyes away. Time to get ready for bed.

Suddenly, Jessica awoke. Had she heard something? What *was* that? She wasn't allowed to keep a modern, digital clock with easy-to-read, glowing numbers near her bed, and her parents took her cell phone away at night, so she didn't know what time it was, but the pitch darkness of the room told her it was late.

Well, it was *almost* entirely dark. From her bed, Jessica could make out the faint sheen of the mirror's glass in the dark.

Tap. Tap, tap. Then silence.

The noise was quiet, subtle, but it still might have been what woke her. Jessica strained her ears. Where was it coming from?

Tap, tap, *tap, tap, tap!* It was getting louder.

Only when the mirror nearly shook on the wall did she realize that the noise was coming from there.

Jessica clutched her comforter tightly around her, trying not to breathe. Maybe whatever it was would stop if it didn't know she was there.

Silence again. Was her plan working?

"Jessica." The single word disturbed the calmness. Spoken in a scratchy, wheezy sigh, the voice almost made her think she was dreaming. But, no, she was wide awake, and something had stated her name.

Something that was not quite human, she realized.

Jessica didn't know if she should answer or continue trying to remain unnoticed. All she knew was the taste of her own terror, bitter in her mouth. The hair on the back of her neck stood on end, and goose bumps broke out on her flesh.

"Come, Jessica." The voice, slightly louder and stronger by now, seemed to be coming back to life, gaining momentum.

"Go away!" she said with as much courage as she could muster, covering her ears with her hands to drown out that incessant demand. "Leave me alone!" She hoped her parents would hear her and come to the rescue. But, at twelve years old, she hadn't needed them in the night for years and years.

"No. You are *mine* now. You have gazed into the mirror," the hollow voice rasped.

A cold shiver ran down Jessica's spine. She felt helpless, trapped.

But it was just a mirror, right? As long as she kept away from it, nothing would happen. She wanted to hide under the covers, but she didn't want anything to creep up on her, just like she didn't want to look at the mirror, but she couldn't take her eyes off of it, either.

And that was when she saw the figure emerge, gray and shadowy, out of the glass. It was a woman, a young woman who might have once been beautiful. Now, with her dead, loose skin and tangled, dirty hair, she was simply horrifying. Very slowly, painfully, she oozed through the mirror until she was standing in Jessica's room.

"Come. You have gazed into the mirror," the figure said, its voice steel. "I will take you now."

Freezing in her bed, unable to move or make a sound as the terrible creature limped closer and closer, Jessica opened her mouth to scream, but no sound materialized. The rotting hands clasped her shoulders and would not let go; Jessica's struggle was of no use. The thing dragged her back to its mirror and crept back inside, no longer alone behind the glass.

***

Six months later, Jessica's parents finally packed up or sold their belongings and moved out. The memories of their lost daughter were too heart-wrenching to remain in their house.

The mirror ended up for sale once again. The Macintoshes couldn't even look at it; the day they bought and hung it was the worst day of their lives, so they wanted nothing to do with it. Mrs. Macintosh even sold it for less than she had paid—that's how much she hated the mirror, never knowing that her daughter, or at least what was left of her, resided inside.

In the back of the antique shop, the original thing, as well as the thing that had once been Jessica, waited patiently to meet their next eternal companion.

THE CIGARETTE-MOUTHED MAN

Charlotte saw him for the first time after her shift at the bar one hazy summer night. In the dim parking lot, she could only make out the orange tip of his burning cigarette and the crisp white of his shirt.

Frowning at this mysterious character who was too close to her car, she reached for her keys and clutched them as a weapon. Perhaps he was some guy sobering up before heading home, a barfly trying to be responsible. But there was always the underlying possibility that this man was *waiting* for her, that he could harm her.

Ever since she took this job, worrying her parents with all the evils that could befall a young woman, she assured them that safety was her number one priority. Men, in general, could be cruel and angry if rejected, and Charlotte's big eyes, full lips, long hair, and ample curves attracted attention, even in her hideous polyester Bulldog Saloon uniform. *Drunk* men, in particular, could be cruel, angry, and, worst of all, unpredictable. Charlotte had promised she would never let her guard down on these late nights.

Get to the car, get to the car, get to the car. She repeated the words in her head, a mantra, planning to make a quick getaway without the shadowy figure's notice. She had heard the cautionary tales of men jumping into women's backseats, so she dared not press the key fob as per usual, not wanting to risk unlocking her car or turning on the lights.

But then another car's headlights flooded the darkness, illuminating the man, bathing him in the radiance.

Charlotte let out a gasp. He was *gorgeous*. Without a doubt, this smoking stranger in his non-descript white tee shirt and jeans was the most handsome man she had ever seen in person, from his broad, muscled shoulders, strong jaw, and closely trimmed, ash blond hair.

His eyes enlarged as she came closer, misinterpreting her reaction. "Sorry. Didn't mean to scare you. Just having a smoke while waiting for my buddy to pick me up." Even his voice, deep with a hint of elsewhere—perhaps a slight Southern twang?—carried his sheer beauty, his confidence emanating through his words. He held out a crumpled pack of cigarettes. "You want one?"

Trying not to inhale any smoke while needing to take a calming deep breath, Charlotte shook her head. "No, thanks. I don't smoke. It's been another long night, so I'm ready to head home." She indicated her uniform, the cartoon dog's head and garish lettering, in case it wasn't clear that she worked at the bar. She hadn't seen him inside and definitely would've noticed, as most of her customers were past fifty and looked like they'd rolled out of Walmart, not a Hollywood set.

He didn't *seem* like a murderer, and he wasn't getting any closer, so she unlocked her car. "Have a good night," she whispered.

"Maybe I'll see you around." He smiled then, his dazzling white teeth reflecting the moonlight, and she drove home to her crappy apartment wondering what would have happened if she had accepted a cigarette, which she hated, simply to enjoy the company of a handsome man for a few more moments, to have some hope in her young life that already seemed diminished of promise and possibility.

***

He was there the next day, as Charlotte had wished, sitting at the bar when she arrived. He glanced up as the door opened, as if he'd been waiting for her.

And he had. His chiseled face broke into a broad grin.

"I was hoping you'd be working tonight." For a moment, Charlotte held back her smile. Did she *really* want to get involved with a guy who visited bars on weeknights, a man who smoked and was low-key stalking her? But then again, maybe he was just being friendly. In the natural lighting, she saw the dimples that accompanied his smile, and she couldn't help but respond.

"Hi." Charlotte took her place behind the bar, searching for a distraction, but there were almost no other customers, and Ben, the bartender she replaced, had high-tailed it out of there as soon as he saw her, anxious to get on with his day.

She grabbed a rag and rubbed it across the already gleaming bar, eager to find something to do so she wouldn't stare at him. "Yep, I'm here almost every night, not in grad school where my parents want me to be." Why did she tell him *that*? She didn't even know his name.

"Charlotte," he said, his eyes on her name tag, which happened to be directly over her left breast. She might have gotten upset at the way his gaze lingered there for a moment, but that's when the light of the setting sun streamed into the room, and his eyes, which she had thought to be brown like hers, a perfectly good color, lit up so she could see that only their sunburst centers, right around the pupil, were a light brown, but the rest of the irises were amber, almost like a wolf's. She didn't ever remember staring into eyes quite like that, those unique colors surrounded by almost black limbal rings.

"Your eyes are beautiful," she said, and her face flushed with embarrassment. Now it seemed like *she* was hitting on *him*.

Again, that devastating smile. "I guess the light must be striking me just right," he said, and she noticed little crinkles in the tan skin surrounding those fascinating orbs. Maybe he was older than she thought, or maybe it was the smoking. She could smell the nicotine on him now, a scent that normally would have repulsed her but was somehow intoxicating when mixed with his cologne and man smell. "Women only tell me that at certain times of the day."

Charlotte's hands stilled, abandoning the rag. She wasn't the *only* woman who had noticed him, and the arrogance of his statement struck her. But when he reached across the bar and touched her hand with his warm, masculine one, an electric charge surged through her whole body. He was tough to ignore, ego or not.

He kicked back the rest of his beer and stood up only a few minutes into their exchange, and Charlotte deflated for a moment. "You get off at eleven, right? I'll be back for you then."

This implication, that she wanted to spend time with him after barely meeting, should have infuriated her. But Charlotte nodded her acquiescence, even though she never did stuff like this and didn't even know this stranger's name. She knew she shouldn't ever give a random man any sort of expectation that she'd go off with him somewhere. She believed in trust, commitment.

Charlotte watched him walk out, and then she waited.

***

Floating through the rest of her shift, nervous, expectant, Charlotte managed to pour wine and pull beers for the various clientele who frequented the establishment. She kept looking at her hand, as if the stranger's powerful touch should have left a mark, maybe even a singe.

He was there waiting for her in the parking lot again, his cigarette glowing in the night. Though she heard her mother's voice in her head telling her not to be so stupid, warning her not to go through with this, that this *wasn't* who she was and she didn't even *know* this man, that it was fine to flirt but *what was she even thinking about doing right now*, she simply pressed the key fob to unlock the door, and he got into her car.

***

Back at her apartment, they fell upon each other the moment Charlotte shut the door. Their limbs entwined as his mouth pressed on hers, tasting of beer and cigarettes. She perceived the brute strength of his arms as he caressed her, and when she couldn't bear it any longer, she grabbed his hand and led him to the bedroom.

Charlotte knew she should put on the brakes. This wasn't like her, not at all. But she was *drunk* on him, stupefied by his magnetism.

When she finally gave all of herself to him, he stared greedily through those golden eyes, and that's when he opened his mouth wide, unhinging his jaw like a cobra. Charlotte saw only cigarette butts instead of those shiny, white teeth, and blackened, charred ends rooted into his gums. He exhaled a thick, black, putrid smoke that swirled out and entered Charlotte through her nose and mouth.

Charlotte felt dizzy, so dizzy, and she couldn't breathe or think anymore. And then Charlotte wasn't Charlotte anymore, and the Cigarette-Mouthed Man took his leave.

***

When the creature that looked like Charlotte got ready to head to its shift at the bar the next day, it put on lipstick before smiling at its reflection. For a moment, its real teeth emerged, the dirty cigarette butts, and a wisp of black smoke crept out from its mouth, encircling its head, but it knew it needed to look pretty for work to find new victims.

TUNNEL VISION

Holding my breath upon entering the snake-like cave, violent images flash through my mind. I try to chase them away and focus on the road ahead of me, the literal light at the end of the tunnel, but the reel won't stop. I envision cars crossing the center line and crashing into each other, shattering glass and crunching metal. I hear the futile screeches of brakes, the shrieks of shock and pain from the passengers as their bodies are crushed on impact. I think what it would be like to get stuck in here with a massive pile up of cars, trapped with demolished vehicles which could ignite into flame, imprisoned with nowhere to go, my fate sealed.

Go straight. Take deep breaths. You're fine; it's fine. You can do this.

I've turned down the music, a perky Lady Gaga song that in no way fits the gravity of my situation, so I'm not distracted.

I hate driving. I hate tunnels. I hate driving through tunnels.

But it's a price I'm willing to pay for freedom.

From the trunk of the car, wrapped in a blue tarp we'd once used for camping, Will remains mum, no longer criticizing my driving. Finally, Will has no words, no words at all.

***

It's not how I planned it, but plans change, just like people. Once upon a time, back in college, Will used to buy me flowers, much to the chagrin of my bitchy roommate whose so-called boyfriend only showed up at our apartment when he was drunk. I don't think he ever even took her to McDonald's. But how does that matter when, according to social media, she's a successful real estate agent who appears happily married? It *doesn't* matter. I need to concentrate on this drive.

And good for her, I guess. Even though she used to steal my food and then claim she didn't, incriminating Cheeto dust still on her fingers, I wouldn't have wished her life to end up like mine.

My cracked rib throbs as this thought flits through my head, a dusty, inconsequential moth compared with the elephant in the room. I have bigger concerns than college roommates.

The drive to the cabin shouldn't be *too* bad, as long as I can navigate my way with this old roadmap I found, having left my phone at home for safety. It's 166 miles from point A to point B, staying away from toll roads to avoid camera and E-ZPass surveillance. According to the Google search I conducted anonymously at the public library, it should only take two hours and thirty-four minutes.

Lies.

Maybe if *Will* was driving that would be accurate, but his driving days are done, his fingers stiffening with rigor mortis, never to grip a steering wheel or grasp my arm. Never again to clench into a fist and punch me in the stomach, where the bruise wouldn't show, when I burned his dinner. He said I could never get a recipe right.

I guess the sleepy-time cocktail I gave him last night was no different. I screwed that up, too, and I'm paying the price once again, albeit not as the victim this time.

***

I've been taking the drive nice and slow, not wanting to risk an accident, or, perhaps worse, a cop pulling me over.

Should I have called the police last night, when I first noticed Will wasn't breathing? How could I, when he was one of their own?

Almost exactly two years ago to the day, that first time Will hit me after what should have been a fun night at the neighbors' house, I called 911. I didn't know what else to do—I'd never seen that side of him, and it was terrifying. This man who promised to love and cherish me in front of all of our family and friends turned into a stranger before my very eyes as I brushed my teeth, thinking the evening had been successful.

I actually *smiled* at him in the mirror before it happened. "So, they're pretty cool, right? Alex and Jed? I know you were nervous that they'd be weird or something, but she's so smart! And kind of funny! And they're both into running, so maybe we could get back into that and do a 5K with them?"

The truth was that Will had put on some weight after college, and I knew he wasn't happy about it based on his huffing and puffing when he said he needed some new pants, but I never would've brought it up. I'd put on a few pounds, too. We weren't kids anymore, and we *could* benefit from being more active.

"We won't be socializing with them again. They're not our kind of people." His voice cold and formal, Will didn't turn his head to look at me, but his dark eyes found mine in our reflections.

"What are you talking about? You acted like you had a great time! And they're awesome! What do you mean?"

"Are you fucking serious, Shay? You told those virtual *strangers* that I had to get back in shape, like I'm some fat asshole."

I'd only had a single glass of chardonnay, but my brain struggled to comprehend Will's words. I spat my toothpaste into the sink and faced him. "Will, I said *we* needed to get back into shape. They're, like, super fit, and I thought it might be fun. We used to run in college together, remember? We used to do a lot of things."

Despite the lack of central air in our Victorian house on the steamy August night, a chill ran down my spine as a montage of "things we no longer did" rushed through me. We no longer ate waffles in bed on Saturday mornings, watched cheesy rom coms, or put thousand-piece jigsaw puzzles together. When had things changed so much?

Had *Will* really changed so much since we got married?

The answer hit me like a punch in the face since it *was* a punch in the face.

After I peeled myself off the tiled bathroom floor, I ran from him, all the way down to the basement to barricade myself in the storage area. Thank goodness my pajama shorts had pockets and that I'd placed my cell phone inside.

Not that it mattered. The cop who responded to my call had attended the police academy at the same time as Will. He'd even come to our wedding. From behind the perceived safety of the thick door, I heard Will claim I'd had too much to drink, and that we'd had a dumb fight since he said our neighbor was pretty.

Steve, the cop, didn't even speak to me. I heard his low chuckle as I slid down onto the cold, concrete floor, defeated.

There was no help for me there.

Not then, and not now.

***

166 miles equals six full marathons plus an almost nine-mile run. Since I had recently run a full marathon, my very first since I had to bow out of an earlier one after another Will-related injury, I tried to trick myself into thinking it was better to drive that distance than to run it. Every 26.2 miles, I imagined another marathon accomplished. This provided minimal comfort, but it helped occupy my mind on something productive.

Even though Will didn't want us socializing, I had started running with Alex a few times a week. As Will's demons grew, I trained my body to run farther and farther. After a few successful half marathons, we kept going.

But running won't save me now. I can't get rid of Will's body by carrying it. I need to drive.

My palms sweating, heart racing, I picture my car spinning out of control. I repeat Hail Marys in my head and pray for my safety.

I've been doing that a lot lately, which is why I decided to leave Will in the first place. I knew he'd never let me go, so my plan was to disappear while he was knocked out. I'd been squirreling away cash for months and had reserved the rental under a false identity, hoping to use it as my home base until I figured out next steps.

But with Will in his condition, *he'll* be the one staying at the cabin. Well, near it, anyway. I'll get to keep my life, my career, my friends, everything I thought I'd have to leave behind.

A smile curls on my lips even though there's so much left to figure out, the main problem being what I'll say has happened to Will.

Maybe the pain from my recent beating messed up my math skills as I calculated the dose to give him. What's done is done, though. There's no turning back.

I finally exit the tunnel, expecting the relief to wash over me. Instead, it's like I'm floating outside of my body, looking down from an aerial view as my car keeps driving straight instead of curving with the road. I see my little red Honda driving right off the cliff, into the abyss, unable to stop. Focusing on bringing myself back to my body, I adjust my hands on the wheel, staying the course.

I need to. I *must* dispose of this evil, dead weight, and make my way back home.

Only 70 miles to go. Only one more hour until I can walk on my own two legs. This is temporary. I can do it.

And when I get there, I'll dig a hole and bury my bastard of a husband in an unmarked grave in the massive woods, praying like hell that I'll get away with it.

FALL

MATKA LOVES YOU

As the grandfather clock chimes four times, the metallic twangs reverberating through the small, neat apartment, Dagmara sits down in her rocking chair.

"Hush, now, sweet girl. Matka will keep you safe. Matka loves you," she says, grasping the stiff, plaster doll to her chest and stroking its silken hair. Dagmara's light blue eyes, though trained on the window, appear almost vacant, unseeing as the sun dips below the horizon in the late autumn afternoon. In its bright, traditional attire, the effigy contrasts sharply with the woman, who is dressed in black with little adornment other than a hint of color on her lips.

"How beautiful you looked that day, your eighth birthday, in your finery. I was so proud of you! And how you danced at the festival. No mother would be prouder of a daughter, with your swinging skirt and shiny hair. That was my best day until it was my worst." Dagmara rocks rhythmically, back and forth, clutching the doll tighter. "All those years ago, yet it feels like yesterday. Your father was a weak man. He had no sense of responsibility. No control."

Dagmara stills, pirouetting the doll around and cradling its head in her hands. "*You* were the one I loved. Love. I love you, my sweet, sweet Adela. If only I had known, I would have stopped it." Her words strangle as sobs course through her body. "I would have crossed heaven and earth to save *you* and crucify *him*. He was a devil, your father, and I hope he rots in hell. I hope he *is* rotting."

She clasps the doll to her chest again, almost crushing its fragile form. "The *policja* spared me the details, what all had happened to you. They brought me your broken body the next day, the day after the festival. After you disappeared. And your father, crying along with me. But I saw the scratches on his arms. I knew *you* put them there."

Dagmara sighs, and the weeping ceases, her breaths slowing as she regains control. "I vowed that very day to avenge you. I waited for him to admit what he had done, to show some sign of his guilt. But he would not, could not. That pathetic, weak *leniwy drainu,* that lazy bastard, slept all night as if he never even lost a little girl—as if he never hurt you. He stood by dry-eyed as they lowered you into the ground.

"So I waited. I waited until that *fatalnie podrywasz*, that lousy drunk, could die in a way that looked natural for a 'grieving' father. It didn't take long. I waited until he drank all the vodka. I led him into the warm bath, and he watched as I slit his wrists with the kitchen knife."

Dagmara pivots her head, her eyes now focusing on the figure in her liver-spotted hands. "As the blood flowed out of his veins, he told me he was sorry. But *I* am not. I am not sorry for what I did to your father. The water turned pink, then crimson, and I slept soundly for the first time in months."

She begins rocking again, caressing the doll. "The *policja* did not question me. Everyone pitied the poor woman who lost her daughter and husband." Dagmara sneers, her normally placid expression distorting into a grimace. "If only I could have thrown your father's body to the pigs."

Rising from her chair and traversing the small room, she places the doll back on the shelf. She puts on her apron, readying herself for her job at the convenience store. It is 4:15.

Dagmara smiles. "Until tomorrow, my sweet Adela. Your matka loves you. Happy birthday."

UNDER THE APPLE TREE

A simple man, Edgar Cummings lived in a cottage with his mother long past the time when others began courting for a wife. He fed the chickens, milked the goat, and helped his mother, day after day and year after year. Broad-shouldered and strong-backed, Edgar earned extra money as a hired hand on the neighboring farm, sowing the corn and reaping the harvest.

After his hearty dinner of meat and potatoes every night, before he lay down to rest, Edgar sat under the apple tree, at least for a few minutes, even when the land rested under a blanket of snow. A quiet man of simple pleasures, he looked out at the sky and counted the stars, shining and distant, as he enjoyed a glass of ale and maybe a few pieces of taffy if wages allowed. Sometimes, his mother joined him.

And so it was, day after day and year after year, and the trajectory of Edgar's life probably would have continued in this vein until he turned old and decrepit. But then the Robertson family moved into the old forge across the way, and everything changed.

The Robertsons slid into the rhythm of village life, adding new and exciting chords to the melody. Mr. Robertson's blacksmith skills became the talk of the town, and men from far and wide traveled to the village to shod their horses with his superior wares. Mrs. Robertson's blackberry pie won the coveted first place prize at the Independence Day picnic, and every lady in town yearned to discover the secret to that recipe. Embraced into the bosom of the community, Mrs. Robertson soon received invitations to sewing circles and Bible study groups. Little Martha Robertson's cherubic cheeks and warm brown eyes radiated sunshine to everyone she passed as she held onto her mother's skirt with her chubby paw.

Once Mr. Robertson met his neighbor, the brawny, taciturn young man who worked like an ox, the parsimonious blacksmith began giving Edgar odd jobs, paying him half what he'd grant another lad. Edgar lacked the mental faculty for the finer skills of the trade, but he took orders and hauled metal and cleaned out horse stalls with nary a grunt or complaint.

Little Martha, shy and quiet herself, adored her neighbor, this gentle giant, and the villagers became accustomed to seeing the two unlikely friends sitting together under the apple tree, large and small, chewing their taffy in companionable silence. Edgar's days had played a single note for many years, but now he embraced this unexpected harmony of friendship. A thirty-year-old man and four-year-old girl: separated by decades and gender, they were yet so similar in their ways.

At dusk one warm, hazy evening in late September, Edgar could scarcely contain his excitement. A new taffy flavor! Peppermint! Little Martha would jump for joy, clapping her hands in delight and giggling in glee. He waited under the apple tree as the sun set.

Night fell, and the stars shone, and *still* she did not come.

Where *was* she? He got up, unwrapping a piece of taffy and popping it into his mouth, to ease his craving and worry.

Edgar skulked through the cornfield and around the smithy, peeking into corners in case Little Martha wanted to play her beloved game of hide and seek. How naughty she was! He looked past the garden and under the haystack. He crept into the stable.

And there he found her, in the horse trough, hiding. Face down, her two yellow braids floating like water lilies. He turned her over, ready to surprise her, but Little Martha's open brown eyes were flat, not warm. Was she sleeping?

Edgar did not know what to do. He wanted his friend to wake up. He picked up Little Martha's cold, wet form and carried her back to her parents' cottage.

He knocked on the door, still chewing his taffy. He hoped Mr. and Mrs. Robertson would help. He wanted Little Martha to come sit under the apple tree with him.

The Robertsons opened their door. When their eyes absorbed the lifeless corpse of their daughter, the Robertsons also did *not* know what to do. They keened and wailed, their family now forever shrouded in grief.

Suddenly, the Robertsons were like wolves, thirsting for blood. They yelled and screamed, shrieked and bawled, and the other villagers appeared, creeping out of the night like mist.

They raged at Edgar. They roared at him, "Killer!"

Edgar's hulking frame seemed to shrink. He *tried* to talk, to say that Little Martha was sleeping and he wanted her to wake up, but his mouth was clogged with taffy.

He gurgled as they grabbed him. He cried and finally screeched, the taffy eventually loosening from his jaws. But it was too late to explain, and the noose was upon him. The villagers hanged him from a branch of the apple tree.

The stars glimmered in the bleak, moonless night, and only his mother mourned him as Edgar's large, lumbering body swung like a pendulum, back and forth until finally still, under the apple tree.

NIGHT SCHOOL

"Now, Drake, I want you to be on your best behavior this time. It's your last chance," Mrs. Anderson told her son before he climbed out of the old station wagon.

"Whatever, Mom, just be here on time to pick me up," Drake muttered in return. He grabbed his nearly-empty backpack, freshly purchased by his mother for his new school.

Mrs. Anderson waved goodbye as her teenaged son shuffled into the building. A large, concrete structure almost glistening in the moonlight, it reminded her of a prison. Of course, that was exactly where Drake was headed if he didn't clean up his act. Expelled from every public school in the area and rejected by the private schools, Drake Anderson was every teacher's worst nightmare, a fact that shamed his mother.

She had hoped and prayed for a son; she really had. Little did she know that, despite loving him as much as a mother could, her sweet, chubby baby would grow into a foul-mouthed, disrespectful juvenile delinquent. She and Drake's father had tried everything, but even Mr. Anderson had given up on his son, packing up his belongings and disappearing one Friday afternoon several years before. Mrs. Anderson and Drake had come home from the principal's office to find nothing but a brief note: "I can't handle the boy anymore. Sorry."

Poor Mrs. Anderson became even more devoted to nurturing her son, thinking she must be at fault for his behavior. In addition to her full-time job at the day care center, she started picking up shifts at the grocery store to pay for parenting classes, searching for ideas on how to reform her son. But nothing worked.

Day after day, Mrs. Anderson received complaints about Drake's behavior. The teachers called and told her about the foul language, talking back, and bullying. The neighbors came over, yelling, demanding she repay them for broken windows and torn-up flower beds. Even the police had called on a few occasions with warnings; Drake had been caught throwing rocks at children on a playground.

No matter what, Mrs. Anderson held out hope that it was all a phase. Her fifteen-year-old son would one day become a contributing member of society. She just had to wait it out; she was sure of it.

But it was barely October when Blackthorn High School called her in for a conference, and she knew Drake was in hot water. Mr. Hamilton, a slight, graying man with a cold voice, calmly explained that, according to the student code of conduct and a vote from the school board, Drake was expelled once again. His vicious threats to a teacher could not be ignored: He was *done*.

"There's nowhere else for him to go," Mrs. Anderson had managed, twisting the handle of her purse as she attempted to keep her tears at bay. "I'm sorry. I just don't know what to do."

Something in Mr. Hamilton's demeanor lightened. Perhaps he pitied this woman who had to raise such an abominable young man. Maybe he understood that she really *was* trying her best at parenting. Maybe Drake was simply a bad seed. "There *is* one place that will still take him," he said. He reached into a drawer on his desk and pulled out a glossy pamphlet.

After hesitating, Mrs. Anderson reached out her hand and took it. "Hemlock Hill Night School? Is this a high school?"

"I only recommend certain students for this program," Mr. Hamilton began in his serious, deep voice, "students like your son. Mostly, the students who attend that school have been, uh, *unsuccessful* in traditional school settings. Hemlock Hill has quite a way of straightening students out." He smiled to himself, thinking about some of his former difficult students and the radical changes that had taken place in them after even a short stint at Hemlock Hill.

"Um, like a military school? A boot camp?" Mrs. Anderson asked, unsure. She had been through the process of switching schools so many times before, only to have her hopes crushed again and again. Drake wouldn't behave *anywhere*.

"I wouldn't say that. But I think you should give it a try. It just might work."

***

Drake Anderson walked into the cool, dark building. It seemed deserted; where were the other students?

"What kind of stupid high school has classes only at night?" he mumbled. He had been told by his mother that one of the school's guiding principles was that students had less aggressive tendencies in the evening, making learning more likely to occur.

Whatever, Drake thought. He didn't remember hearing anything like that in biology class. Oh, right, he probably hadn't been paying attention.

"Drake Anderson," a woman's voice stated. He looked up to see himself staring directly into the eyes of a glamorous woman. Tall, thin, and wearing a tailored black suit, she looked like a model, not like one of the dumpy, potato-bodied teachers he was used to. He must have been so distracted that he didn't even hear her walk up to him.

"Yeah, that's me. What do *you* care?" Though she was extremely beautiful, even that wasn't enough to elicit a polite response from Drake.

"I wasn't asking," she said in her light accent, one he couldn't place. Eastern European, maybe? Her red lips curled into a small smile that didn't reach her cold, gray eyes. "My name is Dr. Kozak. I am the principal here at Hemlock Hill, a school where we do not allow disrespect. You will learn to behave. It is our *way*."

Drake opened his mouth, about to begin one of his usual profanity-laced tirades. In the past, such sentiments would have no effect on him whatsoever—no stupid principal would scare him. Somehow, though, he couldn't form any words, his mind blank of insults and his tongue thick and sluggish in his mouth. He stared, transfixed, at her pale skin and her straight, dark hair.

Dr. Kozak seemed unfazed by Drake's lack of communication. She grabbed his arm by the elbow—not roughly, but not gently either—and led him down the hall. Drake's shoes made dull thuds on the tile, yet Dr. Kozak seemed to glide, soundless.

"Here is your first class of the evening: English, with Mr. Luca. I shall leave you here and *highly* recommend that you do everything he says." With that, she left.

One foot plodding in front of the other, Drake practically stumbled into the classroom. He didn't understand what his problem was; *nothing* got a rise out of him, let alone some stupid lady principal.

Pausing at the doorway, his gaze swallowed the view. At first, it seemed like most of the rooms in the various high schools he had attended: cinder block walls, a whiteboard in the front of the room, a teacher's desk, and about twenty student desks. Something was off, though.

"Ah, Mr. Anderson. We've been expecting you," a man's deep voice drawled.

Drake found himself looking up into two black pools, the eyes of Mr. Luca. Not knowing what to do, he grunted to indicate that, indeed, he was the person who was expected.

"I can tell we must work on sharpening your articulation skills," the teacher said. "We have reserved a seat for you, here in the front. All of the new students must sit in the *front*."

Drake plopped down into the chair, his face burning. He felt embarrassed, but he didn't understand why. What *was* it with these people? He had gone to new schools so many times before, and he had never felt intimidated. He stole a quick glimpse to the side to see the other students, his new classmates. What were they thinking about him? Not that he cared, of course.

Drake had never had any real friends. Whenever someone tried to strike up a friendly conversation, he would lash out and drive them away. But he had always been *noticed*. Now, as he looked left and right, he saw that the two boys sat stone-still with their eyes staring straight ahead, like Drake didn't even exist.

It was only then that he noticed what was different in the classroom: It was completely quiet. No one was laughing or having a conversation with a friend; no one was tapping his pencil; no one was popping gum. No one was moving *at all*, except for their slow, steady breathing. Drake contemplated his new teacher, trying to understand what kind of control this tall, thin, pale man had over them.

Most teachers he knew acted like they wanted to be the students' friends and just fawned all over them with their sappy, overdramatic *caring*. This dude was *not* that type of teacher.

"A question, Mr. Anderson?" Mr. Luca snapped at him.

Drake shook his head. He never listened to teachers; what was wrong with him?

"Well, then, class, you have met our new student. Now please get out your novels."

Obediently, nineteen pairs of hands reached into nineteen backpacks and extracted nineteen books. The only noise was the brief shuffling and the small *tap* on the desk as each book found its mark.

Only Drake failed to produce the novel. He knew his mother had purchased everything he needed, but he didn't care about going to this lame new school and what stupid supplies he needed. Now he wished he had packed his bag with more care.

"Turn to page 59, where we left off," Mr. Luca stated. He surveyed his students for compliance, his black eyes settling upon Drake. "Problem, Mr. Anderson? Already?" The teacher's voice was ice cold.

Drake cleared his throat. "I, uh, forgot my book." He couldn't understand why he felt so small, so insignificant.

"Then we do *indeed* have a problem. We simply don't tolerate any type of misbehavior. And it's one of my favorites we're analyzing, you see. Bram Stoker's classic, *Dracula*." Mr. Luca smiled, showing two rows of perfectly straight, white teeth.

Drake's blood ran cold in his veins as his teacher's fangs emerged from that eerie grin.

***

Several hours later, Mrs. Anderson watched her son hurrying to the car. Anxious to find out how everything had gone, she vowed not to ask any upsetting questions. "Hello, Drake," she said as he got in, bracing herself for his inevitable cruelty.

"Hi, Mom," he replied. "Thanks for getting here on time. I appreciate it. I have some reading to complete to be ready for school tomorrow."

Mrs. Anderson's mouth dropped open in shock. Had Drake ever greeted her politely before, and had he ever talked about doing homework? *Ever?* Those teachers at Hemlock Hill certainly had a way with troubled students.

Indeed, they did.

GLITCH IN THE SYSTEM

I know what you did, Professor Wiggins. The damning words stared out at her, black writing against the white screen, buried in a student's paper in the middle of a sentence analyzing Monday's reading.

Inhaling a sharp breath, Alice peeled her eyes from her computer and looked from left to right, certain someone was playing a cruel trick on her, but all her vision embraced was the kitschy décor of her cat-themed home office: the ticking Kit Cat Klock, imposing Le Chat Noir print, and Japanese waving cat ornament. These were the objects that induced happiness as she burnt the midnight oil grading papers.

The words on the screen, however, failed to elicit any pleasure. Quite the opposite, in fact: her hackles rose in consternation. She glanced at the name on the paper and tried to attach it to a face, but "Jaden Addams" evoked not even a spark of recognition.

Back when she had to play the game of academia to impress the bigwigs and earn tenure, Alice had prided herself on learning her students' names as quickly as possible. Times had changed, though—here it was mid-October, and she didn't have a clue who this Jaden character was.

Maybe he hadn't turned anything in and wasn't attending class? Alice had given up taking attendance long ago. It wasn't required by Blackthorn University, so why should she bother? If students wanted to learn, they would come to class. She couldn't *force* anyone to show up or complete their work. That wasn't her job.

After removing her glasses to rub her eyes, Alice clicked out of the document without making any comments. While she had initially loathed the switch from paper to electronic submissions, she found she could cycle through her grading faster this way, copying and pasting canned comments that these kids probably weren't reading anyway. With that AI thingamajig her department chair kept harping on about, who knew if they were even writing their own papers anymore.

As she inched toward retirement—and she was close, with only one more year to go until she could collect full benefits—the less Alice cared. This younger generation wasn't worried about behaviorism or cognitive theories; they were too concerned about their Instagram followers and whatever was trending on TikTok. Alice had never bought into that social media nonsense. She was pretty disconnected from *much* of what was going on at the university these days; that was the cold, hard truth of the matter. She couldn't be bothered.

But the words in Jaden's paper, *these* she cared about. Who was he, and, more importantly, how did he *know*? That business had concluded long ago, the inquest having resulted in condolences rather than punishment. As far as anyone knew, Alice was blameless, a victim and unwilling pawn in what had spiraled into a senseless act of violence.

And the one who *did* know exactly what Alice had done wasn't in a position to breathe a word of his involvement. In fact, he wasn't in a position to breathe at all, his life long since extinguished.

***

Alice stifled a yawn as the students shuffled out of the classroom the next morning. She'd stayed up too late the night before, looking through Jaden's previous submitted work, and found him to be an average student without any reason to cause problems. But how could she give him a grade for a paper containing such an intrusive and threatening comment? While Alice's normal approach with troublemakers was to report them to the dean, she thought this case might need to be handled in a different, more confidential manner.

"Dr. Wiggins? You said on my paper you wanted to see me?" A tall, thin boy slouched in front of the lectern: the elusive Jaden.

"Yes." Though she longed to complete this encounter and retire back to the sanctuary of her office alone, where she was unlikely to be bothered, students from the next professor's class were already clamoring near the door to get in. "Please follow me to my office so that we can talk."

"Okay, but I—" Alice's withering glare cut Jaden's words short, and he followed her into the hallway and up the stairs.

Alice took her time, refusing to rush to keep up with this boy's long strides, fumbling to gather her office keys in her bag, and settling her belongings once inside her office. *Let* him wait. He'd caused her enough hassle as it was, and she would draw this out as long as necessary if it meant she could gain the upper hand.

Finally, she began. "I suppose you know why I've called you in here."

Jaden scratched at an angry, red pimple on his chin, his face blanching. "I guess you didn't like my paper? I kinda struggled with the reading. You know, that Skinner guy is pretty tough, but I didn't cheat, if that's what you think. Honest." He swallowed, his Adam's apple bobbing up and down like the strength tester at a carnival.

"It's what you wrote *within* your paper. What you hid there. I want to know why you would say something so utterly inappropriate." Though careful not to overplay her hand, Alice needed to find out what this cretin wanted.

Jaden's heavy eyebrows arched into peaks. "Oh my god, did I use a bad word? If I did, I'm sorry. It must have been a typo."

"Let's take a look at exactly what you wrote. What you wrote to *me*. And then let's talk about why," Alice said, her voice flinty. Logging into the learning management system, she opened up Jaden's latest offering and swung her monitor around to face him.

Jaden squinted, mouthing the words as he reread the page. "Professor, I like, literally don't know what you're talking about."

Alice pursed her lips, exhaling through her nostrils. "I don't understand how you would muster up the audacity to write such a thing and then not have the courage to talk to me about it." Spinning the monitor back around, she searched for the objectionable sentence, one she had unearthed so easily the night before.

But it was gone, and all that remained offensive in Jaden's writing was his frequent use of run-on sentences.

"I don't understand how you did this." Alice heard the tremor in her voice.

"I'm sorry, Professor, but I really don't know what you're talking about, and I need to go to my next class. Is that okay? Are *you* okay? Do you need some water, or do you want me to get someone?"

As Alice met Jaden's gaze, rather than defiance, she saw compassion, maybe pity, in his dark eyes. She waved him off. "I'm sorry," she managed, her voice thin and strangled. "I'll take another look at your paper and give you some feedback."

Closing the door behind him and turning down the glaring fluorescent lights, Alice collapsed into her ergonomic chair to massage her temples, willing the growing pressure in her head to dissipate. She'd seen those words; she knew she had.

Maybe Jaden had somehow retracted his earlier paper and resubmitted? But the submission window was closed. And he really *had* seemed genuine, unless he was an accomplished actor, and she'd checked his student profile to see that he was a business major, not theatre. Maybe a hacker was taunting her? Whatever it was, whoever was doing this, Alice needed to quell it. She was *not* going to allow this to happen to her, not now, not all these years later.

She called the IT help desk and explained that a student's paper had changed after he submitted it.

"No way. It couldn't have happened. The university invested in a high-level security system to prevent data leaks." The man droned on and on, something about "malware" and "ransomware," but Alice had trouble following. "Is it possible that you were mistaken in what you saw, ma'am? Or could you at least be more specific about *what* you saw?"

"It's Dr. Wiggins, and the wording itself is inconsequential," Alice hissed, annoyed by the second implication that morning that she was a person to be pitied. "I *know* the paper was changed."

"Well, *Dr. Wiggins*, perhaps you're right. Perhaps there's something new going on, a glitch in the system. Have a good day now." He hung up before Alice could say anything else.

A glitch in the system. She'd heard those words before—she'd even used them herself to explain the unexplainable.

Long ago.

Having experienced enough nonsense for one day, Alice was ready to go home. Even though she technically had office hours for another hour and a half, students rarely showed up. Alice didn't bother including her availability on her syllabus; the ones who really wanted help could contact her, and the others didn't deserve her time. A department meeting was scheduled for later in the afternoon, but she doubted she'd be missed. Many of these younger professors, with their "woke" ways and silly "student-centered approaches," failed to appreciate the wisdom and experience she brought to the table. Just because times changed didn't mean she had to reinvent the way she taught, and she was sick of hearing about it. Who cared about her low evaluations? She was a tenured, full professor with nothing to worry about other than coasting to retirement. Who was going to give *her* any trouble, when there were so many others trying to rock the boat?

Unless, of course, someone really *was* trying to bring up the past. Now *that* could be an issue.

***

Alice needed a break from the stress, so she fixed herself a salad and cup of chamomile tea before settling on the couch to watch soap operas for most of the afternoon. Near dinner, she summoned the energy to feed her two black cats, Suspect and Criminal, and opened her laptop to check her email. She wanted an excuse in hand just in case she was chastised for skipping that department meeting.

And there it was, almost like before, a threat sandwiched in between the words of an otherwise innocuous sentence from her department chair:

While I'm sure there is a reason for your absence, please remember that monthly department meetings are mandatory for all You will be punished, Professor, for what you did *psychology faculty, Alice, and I hope you will provide me with advance notice if you must miss a scheduled meeting in the future.*

Alice's eyes widened. Without the earlier incident, she might have thought her chair had mixed feelings about her truancy, but two messages couldn't be a coincidence. Ralph was a spineless man who was chair only because no one else wanted the position, and Alice doubted he had punished anyone in his life for failing to follow orders.

Could this be about something else, a silly prank from a disgruntled and technologically-savvy student? Maybe she should look over other members of her roster to see if there were any computer science majors in her Psych 101 class.

But if anyone wanted to cause trouble for her, there was one event and one event only that would destroy her if the truth came out.

***

Alice remembered how it had all transpired over thirty years ago, back when her hair was blonde versus gray, her figure years from the inevitable middle-aged spread. She could picture the teased bangs, pegged jeans, and flannel shirts of her students, hear the grunge and R&B music blasting from ubiquitous boom boxes peppering the quad.

There was so much pressure to establish herself as an academic back in those early days at the university. With classes to teach, committees on which to serve, and students to advise, Alice hadn't completed much scholarship at the beginning of her career. When her research study didn't provide statistically significant results, she knew it hampered her chances of publication.

So she fudged some data. Tweaked, more like it, just transposed a few numbers for a bigger effect size. No one would ever notice.

Alice had admitted to herself back in her grad school days that she didn't have either the smarts or drive to become a top researcher in her field, but she needed to publish *some*where. A third or fourth tier journal would be good enough to help her earn tenure but probably wouldn't scrutinize her research to the same degree as a more prestigious publication.

And no one would have been the wiser if not for her meticulous undergraduate research assistant.

Tommy, a senior psych major assigned to Alice for an independent study, had been a godsend when it came to helping code the data, and Alice had come to rely upon him for his proofreading skills.

What she wasn't expecting was how seriously he took his responsibilities.

"Dr. Wiggins? You didn't send the article to the journal yet, did you?" Tommy, dark circles under his eyes, had knocked on her office door—her original office at Blackthorn University, barely bigger than a broom closet—almost as soon as she arrived at work on that crucial morning.

Alice rearranged her face into a mask of surprise. He *couldn't* know. "Why do you ask? Yes, I sent it."

Tommy plopped his backpack right on her desk and began rummaging through it, pulling out folders and papers. "I kept thinking that something was off. I was lying in bed last night, thinking about it, thinking something got messed up somewhere. Look." He pointed his finger at a table listing a much smaller effect size than that which had made it into the final draft of her manuscript.

"Well, that can't be right, Tommy. The results were much higher than that. I reviewed them myself. Maybe the printer messed up, or there was a glitch in the system. You know all the trouble we've had with technology."

They went back and forth for a bit, Alice claiming that the papers were incorrect, Tommy explaining he didn't want her to get in trouble for submitting false data.

"Tommy, I hope you're not insinuating that I'm doing anything unethical," Alice said. She stood up from her desk, back ramrod straight. She would *not* let him destroy the meager foundation of her scholarship. "Hand over those papers. As an undergraduate student rather than the principal investigator, you shouldn't have those in your possession." She extended her hand.

"Dr. Wiggins, I'm trying to help you. That's all I want to do," Tommy said, his expression pained.

Alice grabbed Tommy's backpack, extracting the rest of the folders and papers and clutching them to her chest. Tommy reached out to retrieve them, yanking hard, and Alice fell to the floor, her head thwacking against the side of her desk.

"Oh my god, oh my god," Tommy chanted, dropping to his hands and knees to help her. With her back turned, he didn't see Alice's mouth curl into a smile, but he heard her scream, as did everyone else in the office suite.

In the descending chaos, Alice watched, makeshift icepack on her head, as the campus police officer walked Tommy out in handcuffs. Her colleagues hung around, mouths agape, at the skirmish. Though the officer had taken Tommy's backpack, Alice had swept the printouts out of sight, under her desk. She would shred them later.

In the investigation that followed, Alice kept her story simple. "The student demanded I credit his name as a co-author on the paper, but he hadn't contributed much more than proofreading and data entry, so I told him that was inappropriate. Unfortunately, he became violent."

As far as Alice knew, Tommy didn't accuse her of anything. Or, if he did, no one took it seriously.

Even though Alice opted not to file charges, Tommy was immediately suspended from the university, his scholarship revoked. A formal board hearing had been scheduled to review Tommy's case and determine whether he should be expelled from Blackthorn, but the hearing was canceled.

There was no need to determine Tommy's future. Within a week of the incident, Tommy's landlord, having heard what sounded like a gunshot, keyed into his off-campus apartment to find Tommy lying in bed, his brains splattered across the wall.

His suicide note was short, to the point, and grammatically correct, if not inventive in semantics: *I am deeply sorry for the trouble I have caused.*

Despite how shaken she was from all of it, Alice published her research study and went on to receive tenure. The situation was tragic, of course, but she couldn't take responsibility for Tommy's violent actions, not the push that resulted in her mild concussion and certainly not for his rash decision to end his young life.

***

Having tossed and turned all night, thinking about the disturbing messages she had received, Alice slept through her alarm and didn't have time to put on makeup, style her hair, or drink her tea.

Alice walked in a daze across campus, failing to notice the golden-hued leaves fluttering to the ground in the gentle breeze. For Alice, there was little beauty to be found, only danger, ugliness.

She went straight to her classroom, not even stopping at her office. If her students noticed her distraction or unkempt appearance, no one said a word. Then again, they were a particularly disengaged bunch of freshmen, few of whom were even psych majors. Most of these kids were there to satisfy general education credits, not actually to learn.

Clicking to the next slide of her PowerPoint, Alice continued instruction in her monotone voice. She'd given this lecture so many times, she could recite it by rote. She glanced up at her slide out of habit, and that's when she saw it, projected on her screen for all her students to see: a crime scene photograph of Tommy's suicide.

His long limbs splayed, head tilted back, jaw slack, and eyes vacant, Tommy's ruined body slumped in bed in front of a wall slicked with blood and gray, sponge-like chunks of his brain matter. But worst of all, in what she recalled as Tommy's careful, cramped handwriting, were the words that accompanied the photograph: *Look what you made me do, Dr. Wiggins.*

Gasping in horror, Alice grabbed the remote control, turned off the projector, and faced her students. Most of them had their heads down, buried in their phones. "Class is dismissed!" she yelled, grabbing her purse and running from the room as fast as she could.

She didn't have a plan, but she needed to get away. That's all she cared about now. She needed to get home where she felt safe.

It was a short drive home, thank goodness, but Alice seemed to get stuck behind every red light. She floored it at the intersection once it turned green, not checking whether the coast was clear.

She never saw the tractor trailer coming and barely felt the impact as her car and body were crushed by the much larger vehicle. She didn't hear the screech of metal or her own final scream, cut short as her spinal cord separated from her body.

Later, once the wreckage was cleared, the policeman took statements from the witnesses.

"I was right behind her, officer. I saw the light turn green, but the other light hadn't turned red, or even yellow. They were both green at the same time, I swear. It wasn't the trucker's fault," a witness said. He pointed at the portly man being treated by an EMT in the back of an ambulance.

The officer wrote down the witness's statement. "Must've been a glitch in the system," he said.

WHEN THE TRUTH COMES CRASHING DOWN

It was Sunday, that nonentity of a day between the freedom of Saturday and the harsh reality of Monday, with all its responsibilities and expectations. A day of preparation, filled not *at* work but with it—laundry, grocery shopping, meal prepping, and bill paying.

When April, my best friend, texted me about brunch at a local bar, I replied that I had too much to do. My phone rang about two seconds later. Against my better judgment, knowing how persuasive she could be, I answered.

"There's a band, and they're right up your alley," she said, skipping hello. "It'll take you five minutes to walk here, and I'll buy you your first mimosa. And it's the weekend! You're divorced, not dead."

Ouch. Another reminder to stop hiding out in my apartment like a hermit. In the three months since the paperwork was signed and my simple gold band tossed into the Atlantic Ocean, I hadn't gotten out much.

I peeled myself out of bed, threw some product in my hair, and applied mascara.

I'll stay an hour, I told myself, *and then I'll come home and get to business.* April was right—I needed to start living my life again. My chores could wait.

After a brisk walk in the chilly fall air, I arrived at the Bulldog Saloon, a dimly lit place with a confusing theme. Sports memorabilia and a few animal heads lined the faux brick wall in stark contrast to the hipster items on the menu: acacia mojitos and vegan cupcakes, for instance. I imagined the owners hadn't been able to agree and decided to compromise with this bizarre mishmash.

I spotted April right away. As usual, she stood out from the crowd; while others looked a little grungy like me, April wore a lavender dress that contrasted perfectly against her glossy red hair—effortlessly elegant, while I could barely pull myself together.

She looked up, and I learned this wasn't a casual brunch.

"I need to tell you something," she said, and that's when it happened.

With a loud crash, the tremendous elk head fell from the wall, smashing the glass table beneath it, scattering coffees, muffins, and people.

Shrieks and cries filled the room. As I looked across the table, the tableau unfurled in front of me: April's outstretched hand, the ultrasound picture curled in her fingers. The large, jagged shard of glass jutting out of her pale throat.

Her red blood spilled out from the wound like paint from a can as her mouth opened and closed, opened and closed, and the light went out of her eyes.

When the ambulance came to take her away, I saw him: Lou, my ex, wailing over April's lifeless form, her blood besmirching the light blue sweater I had bought him for Christmas last year.

If he saw me, he didn't acknowledge it. We hadn't parted on good terms after the stress and struggle of our failed attempts at IVF.

He must have been listed as her next of kin. *Someone* had called him. I sat back and watched as April's body got carted away with Lou's dying or dead baby inside of her.

I thought about the betrayal, not just of my own fruitless womb but of my very best friend planning a family with my former partner.

As I walked back to my apartment, friendless, husbandless, and childless, I thought about my chores. There was that laundry to do. I glanced down and wondered if I had solvent to attack the red stain marring my cardigan.

RUN!

"Why do we keep doing these damn things?" Jed grumbled, hunching over to retie his shoelace. "It's cold, and we're gonna get dirty. You *hate* being cold and dirty."

"It'll be fun," I said, my feigned enthusiasm coming out flat. "The Sams love this stuff. It's been a tough year for them, so I think we can suck it up and do a zombie-themed 5K." My sister and her husband—known collectively as The Sams for their same first name—had recently closed their restaurant, the business they had poured their hopes, dreams, and finances into for the past eight years. The least we could do was run through a field with a bunch of other idiots while people decked out as the undead chased us. "Let's just try not to hurt ourselves. My half marathon's next month, and I don't want to mess that up."

Sam and I were both runners, but she preferred races that involved costumes and beer, while I was more interested in earning a new PR and avoiding hitting the wall. Known back in high school as the fun sister, Sam was the life of the party, a social butterfly at ease in every situation, always ready to crack a joke or take on a silly dare. Meanwhile, I was the serious one, staying in to do trigonometry homework on Friday nights while my little sister hung out with the popular kids at parties. I didn't even go to my senior prom since it was the night before a big track meet, but Sam, as a sophomore, had attended. But now Sam and I were *both* the serious ones, her carefree attitude having vanished along with her life savings.

Jed wrapped his arms around me and rested his chin on my head. "You're right. I'll try to have fun." My husband preferred action or comedy, but Sam and I lived for the jump scares in horror movies. It *would* be fun, dammit, putting ourselves into the scene rather than just watching it.

"Stop it with the PDA, you pervs!" a man's voice bellowed across the sea of parked cars. I extricated myself in time to see my brother-in-law, his frame towering over those of other runners, walking toward me. "The Sams have arrived!"

I plastered a big smile on my face and waved, mustering up some excitement. I hadn't seen my sister in person since her announcement last month, and I didn't want my expression to propel her into a downward spiral. "Hey, guys! Cute shirts!"

Sam laughed, gesturing to the tie dyed and bedazzled disaster on her chest. "You like? I thought I'd go for something understated."

"The matching shirts were *my* idea," Sam the man said, reaching out to Jed for their customary bro hug. "Let the world know that we are The Sams!"

They seemed upbeat, but I couldn't help but notice the dark circles under my sister's eyes. If she wanted to pretend everything was okay, though, while she nursed her wounds and figured out next steps, I could play that game. We were here to screech like little kids while some teenagers in heavy makeup chased us, not to be miserable in the harsh reality of adult life. I checked my watch. "Let's head down to the starting point."

***

Clustered with all the other runners, it seemed like any other race at first. People squatted and stretched, adjusted headphones and Garmin watches, and waited. We'd already pinned on our numbered bibs and hung cloth belts around our waists, each with three life flags—the "zombies" would try to grab these, and once they'd gotten all three we were considered dead. If we made it to the finish line with any flags remaining, we would earn special survivor medals.

I rubbed my arms, the chill autumn air biting through my thin nylon sleeves. Maybe I should've made more of an effort. Like The Sams, others wore matching team shirts or even full costumes. I had asked Jed if he wanted to do something together, but he wasn't interested. The guy in the panda suit would stay warm, at least, but I couldn't say the same for the chubby dude in the fluorescent green Borat-style mankini.

"I am *not* running behind that guy," Jed whispered as he walked by us, hairy butt cheeks on display.

"I can't see any zombies from here," my sister said. "I wonder if they'll pop out at us and actually run and chase us."

"Real zombies don't run," her husband answered. "It wouldn't be realistic. So I don't know *how* they're gonna catch us. Maybe some people will just walk and be easy targets. But I'm ready to sprint if any mofo gets near me."

"'Real' zombies?" Jed repeated, hooking his fingers into air quotes. "That's why I don't think this'll be scary. There's no such thing as zombies. If Michael Myers and, I don't know, like Jeffrey Dahmer or someone was chasing me, or a bear maybe, *then* I might get scared. Serial killers exist. Dangerous animals exist. Zombies don't."

"Come on, Jed. Be a good sport. I need to have some fun after all the bad stuff that's gone down, so for once I wasn't pissed to find out my wife had spent money on something without asking me," my brother-in-law said. "This race was kind of expensive, but I'm stoked."

He sounded lighthearted enough, but I glimpsed the clench of his jaw. Was he blaming my *sister* for what happened with the restaurant? This was news to me, especially after she had told me that *he* was the one who opted to switch their supplier to a shady company that ultimately absconded with their payment, leading to their financial ruin.

"Runners, take your marks and listen for the air horn!" My concerns were interrupted by the voice of the announcer, followed by the sharp blast that set the crowd into motion—very *slow* motion due to the tightly-packed bodies. With high knees and little forward movement, I began a sluggish jog, seeking to carve out some personal space for myself.

"Maybe we should stay together?" my sister asked, her voice reedy. "I feel—I don't know, kind of scared, actually."

"You bet," I answered. The four of us had done tons of 5Ks before, and we generally split up, each running at our own pace, not being held back or dragging one another down. But Sam seemed kind of fragile, and the fact that we'd be climbing over and under obstacles and swimming through a stream meant I wouldn't be earning a PR as it was.

"Alex, you and your sister can run together, and that frees us guys up to surge ahead," Jed said.

Jed had never beaten me in a single race, ever, but *okay*. "Sure," I said, holding back the annoyance I felt as I watched the two men take off in front of us, nearly elbowing an older lady in a Wonder Woman costume out of the way.

My sister and I jogged for a few minutes, most of the other runners close at our heels, as the sounds of crunching gravel and heavy breathing punctuated the silence. "If we stick in the middle of a group like this, I bet we'll be protected from the zombies," I said, trying to focus on the positive. I normally hated crowds, but it could work to our advantage this time.

Sam was quiet for a moment. From my sideways glance, I watched her craning her neck. "I can't see the guys anymore, and I *still* don't see any zombies."

From inside the huddle, with most of the other runners dwarfing me with their superior heights, my views were limited, as well. But, when the crowd thinned, the landscape spread out before us, rolling green hills and a cloudless blue sky. We entered the woods as golden leaves descended from above, coating our path in autumnal splendor.

"It's a beautiful day for a run," I said, my voice comfortable in this slower-than-normal jog. "I'm happy we're together for this."

"Me, too." She said it softly and wiped her eye with her hand, but maybe she had an itch.

"Are you okay?"

Before she could answer, a bloodcurdling shriek resounded through the forest.

"The zombies are here!" someone shouted in exhilaration or fear.

A handful of moaning creatures crept out from behind the trees, arms flailing. Moving faster now from the burst of adrenaline that coursed through my veins, I didn't get a good look, but I noticed the filthiness of them, their stringy hair, like they really *had* been decomposing for months rather than made up to look that way. And whoever the company had hired as zombies were committed to their roles—the grunts and snorts sounded legit. I hoped these actors were getting paid well.

The posse cornered a blonde girl about twenty feet away and ripped off her flags, one after the other. "I'm already dead!" she screamed, laughing.

"We are *not* dying before we get to the first mile marker," I said, seizing Sam's arm and trying to get her to speed up.

We ran hard, not talking, leaving behind the slower and weaker, until we entered a clearing with about a dozen other runners. Without discussing it, we all slowed down to a walk.

Nervous laughter rippled amongst us.

"That was kind of terrifying," some guy said. "I got away, but they got one of my flags."

I darted my eyes right and left, searching for hidden zombies, my heart still racing even though I'd escaped unscathed. But the meadow lay calm and still before us. We could breathe for a minute.

"Hey, Alex!" Jed's voice cried. The guys were only a short distance ahead of us. Sam and I charged forward to catch up.

"That was crazy," Sam said when we reached them, his deep voice giddy. "I still have all my flags, baby." He wiggled his hips to shake them.

"Let's keep going," my sister said. "I'm nervous for the next assault."

We trudged on, blending into another group, and reached the first obstacle, a huge, almost vertical wooden ramp with a rope on it.

"This is supposed to be *challenging*?" Sam bounded over to it with his long-legged gait, easily finding his footing, hauling himself up and over as if it were almost nothing. Jed followed his lead with only a little less self-assurance.

My turn. I clasped onto the rope and tried to wedge my foot in the space between the boards, but I was a little too short. Beside me on another rope, my longer-limbed sister managed better.

"Come on, Alex, grab my hand," she said, one hand on her rope and the other reaching out. "We can do this."

My left hand burning from friction, my body tense and ready for battle, I stretched out to her. Slowly, haltingly, we scaled the ramp and jumped down the other side into a shallow but muddy pit, clumps of icy sludge splashing up onto our faces and into our hair.

Our husbands were nowhere in sight, but I caught movement from the corner of my eye. "Sam, they're coming!" A zombie rushed at us, his fingertips grazing my shoulder. "Run!" I pushed back at him, my palm digging into his soft stomach, as I linked my arm into my sister's and took off at a sprint.

We kept on like that for a couple of minutes, our breaths coming out fast and ragged, until the caterwauling and groaning of the creatures subsided.

"They must have been hiding, waiting for us," Sam said, sounding rattled. "Kind of a dirty trick."

"This is way scarier than I thought it would be," I admitted, "but I guess it's what we signed up for. I know it's fake and everything, but I feel petrified each time I see one of them. And I hope I wasn't too rough with that kid—I just didn't want him to steal our flags!"

"Look who's here." Sam's voice came out hollow, emotionless. She gestured to our husbands, the men who said they wouldn't stick together with us, yet we had caught up once again.

"I see you two are no longer intact," I said, eyeing their belts.

"Yeah, they bum-rushed us after the ramp," Jed said, clamping a hand on my shoulder. "How the hell are *you* two whole?"

"We ran like hell," my sister answered. "Don't count us out. And we all know that Alex kicks the rest of our asses at every 5K, so don't be so surprised."

"Yes, your lawyer sister is *so* impressive, so much more so than your loser husband who isn't even the one at fault for losing the business. *I'm* not the one who was always donating money to causes and giving away free meals. We were supposed to be *earning* money, not running a charity," the male Sam responded.

My face flamed in anger and embarrassment. I hadn't realized how tense things had gotten between The Sams, but he didn't need to drag *me* into it. "Let's keep going," I said, just as another cry broke out. I swear, some people were like zombie alarms.

I picked up the pace and nodded for my sister to do the same. The guys followed suit, and we joined the tail end of a mass of runners through a pumpkin patch. Wherever the zombies had been hiding, they were out now, a dozen or more crouching and leaping as runners yelped and evaded their clawing hands.

All of a sudden, I felt hands on my back thrusting me straight into the path of a snarling zombie who swiped a flag from my waist. Screaming, ripping myself away before the young female zombie could inflict more damage, I looked behind me. "Jed? Did you seriously just *push* me?"

"Sorry, babe!" Jed grinned and tapped his waistband. "I was already down a flag, but you could spare one! I had to sacrifice you to save myself! Thanks!"

I kept going, pumping my limbs to endure the chaos, my eyes trained for my sister. Thankfully, I recognized her tie-dyed shirt in the distance—she had made it.

In my short time on the course, I had learned that the zombies didn't chase once you left their area. They stuck to their ground. It must've been one of the rules of the 5K so all the runners got their money's worth of zombie saturation.

"I want to be done. This is too stressful," my sister said once our breathing had steadied. "I know it's fake and everything, but I'm ready for the finish."

"Oh, no," I said, for in front of us trickled a small stream, and there appeared to be no way to circumvent it. I watched as runners waded in, tentatively, and swam their way across to dry land.

The guys didn't hesitate—they leapt right in. "Come on, ladies!" Jed yelled. "Grow some balls!"

"That's a weird thing for my husband to say!" I stepped in, feeling the frigid water engulf my feet and then legs. I imagined hands grasping me and pulling me down into a watery grave, even though I knew that, logically, the so-called zombies were just actors hired for the event. They wouldn't be submerged.

There's no real danger here, I told myself as the murky water crept past my waist.

Another shriek of terror. I was getting used to them by now, but this particular one was too familiar.

"Help! Something has me!" male-Sam shouted. "It's *biting* me!"

Something rose out from the water next to him, something fetid and foul that did *not* look like the product of a special effects department, even a very talented one.

"Sam!" he wailed as the brute chewed his shoulder and moved on to his throat. "Help!" His voice faded as the zombie gnawed. A crimson tide spurted out of my brother-in-law's neck.

Mere yards away, I treaded water as Sam, a man I had known since senior year of college, collapsed into the stream.

"Go. Go! Let's get out of here!" my sister yelled. "I'm putting myself first for once! He said I always put everyone else before myself, that *I'm* the reason the business failed, but let's get out *now!*"

My arms and legs straining, my body rigid with cold and shock, I reached the other side of the stream. Looking back, I couldn't see the other Sam or his assailant anymore.

"Is this real?" I managed. "Did that just happen?"

Sam's harsh, guttural sobs told me that it was. "I think this isn't pretend anymore," she said.

Jed shivered in front of us, his eyes wide and body convulsing, his lips parted as he struggled for air. "What *literally* just happened? Is Sam okay? Is this part of the prank?"

"I don't think it's fake," I said, tears streaming down my face, unsure how to process what I witnessed. "Something's wrong. I *know* that something's wrong here. We need to *go*."

My sister's face paled. "Did I just watch my husband die? What is *happening* here?"

"Keep moving; let's get out of here," I said. "Maybe it's not real, and he's in on it, but we could be putting ourselves in danger if we wait to find out." Behind us, other runners tried to cross only to be pulled down by the beasts in the water.

My eyes widened as I stared ahead at a trio of runners being ambushed by several attackers who were uninterested in their flags. No, these zombies wanted far more. The first two runners eluded their predators, but the zombies brought down a woman whose howls of agony amplified, then subsided, and finally ceased as they bit into her flesh. They knelt in front of her and dipped their heads again and again, coming back for second and third helpings. Reaching into the cavity they had chewed into her body, one of the undead pulled out the woman's tube-like intestines, which he then held in both hands and bit into like a thick, juicy hamburger. Even from as far away as we stood, we could hear the munching and slurping along with sighs of contentment.

No, these were not actors. Whatever had happened in the short time since the race started, this was real.

"Look." Jed pointed with a shaking finger to some scattered corpses, one of which was wearing a red STAFF shirt. "I think they're starting to reanimate."

I watched with dread as the bodies jolted and twitched, like an electric current surged through their dead veins.

"Let's make a run for it now, before those ones get up, and while those others are distracted," Sam said, her voice flinty with resolve. Even though she had been frightened earlier, Sam had found her strength in this catastrophe. "Our cars are parked around the bend from the finish line. Sam had our keys, so I'll go with you guys, and we'll drive away. We'll call for help once we're safe. We're defenseless and can't be heroes here."

Jed and I nodded in acquiescence, ready to follow orders. We bolted past the feasters and around the bin of ice rather than through it—we were running for our lives at this point rather than to earn any stupid participant medal.

"It's there! The finish line!" I paused my stride to point. Only a few runners had made it and were already scampering to their own cars. Like us, they must have realized that there would be no afterparty with food, beer, and music; the instruments and carcasses from the band littered the field in front of us.

"Alex! Jed! Watch out!" Sam yelled, and I turned my head to the right to see a zombie barreling toward me at a speed commiserate with that of a runner. Then again, based on his bib and sneakers, that's what he'd *been* until very recently. His jaw hung slack as he growled at me.

I already knew the feeling of Jed's hands on my back, so I dove left at the first touch. Without me to buffer him, my husband of more than a decade fell straight into the zombie's path. I heard the crunch as it bit into the side of his face and chewed the cartilage of his ear. His warm, wet blood sprayed onto my face.

"I do *not* choose to sacrifice myself!" I hollered as I ran away with my sister. I couldn't bear to watch the light fade from his eyes, or, worse yet, see him reawaken as one of these monsters.

Hot tears cascaded down my face as I thought of the good times we had shared, those lazy Saturday mornings lounging in bed and the vacations to the Caribbean and Europe. But other memories surfaced, as well, as I pushed my arms and legs to their limit. The nights I stayed up waiting for Jed to come home, positive he'd been in a car wreck, but then he'd stumble in smelling of booze and cheap perfume. Or the time he hadn't shown up to the party my parents held when I passed the bar exam—he'd had a scheduling conflict, he said, even though he never explained what it was. The worst was when I checked our joint account, one in which we had been saving for our dream house, to find it drained; Jed's only excuse was that he'd made a poor investment and needed the funding for his next venture.

Was that the sum of my marriage? Had my husband even loved me? Well, it was over now.

We almost threw ourselves onto the hood of my Prius, gasping for breath, our limbs sore but attached to our living bodies. The automatic locks popped open. "Thank God Jed always made me hold onto the keys so he didn't have to bother," I said, tapping the tiny inside pocket of my leggings, where I kept the key fob.

We hurled ourselves inside and locked the doors. "Drive," Sam commanded. "Get us the fuck out of here." My sister never swore, but it had been quite a day.

Nodding, numb with physical and emotional fatigue, I pulled the car out of the mostly full grassland. Few runners had escaped the bloodbath.

After calling 911 and apprising the incredulous dispatcher of the massacre, agreeing that we'd come to the station but would not set foot back on the course lest we end up like the others, we drove on in silence for several minutes.

"Huh," Sam said. I looked to my right to see her gazing down at her shirt. "Jed's blood must have splattered me when he got killed. It's covering the second 's' in The Sams."

"You are now *The* Sam. You are just Sam," I said. We continued on, away from our undead spouses, as the sun set, the pink and red hues bleeding into the October sky.

HOUSE OF SCREAMS

One dark eyebrow raised, Zach looked at his girlfriend. "You know this is stupid, right? Can't we just turn around and go to the movies or something?" He focused his attention back on the road.

Running her fingers through her long, curly hair, Julie said, "Come on. It'll be fun. And Bobby and Andrea are meeting us there. Aren't you always saying you want to do something different?"

Zach sighed, frustrated that he always caved in to Julie's demands. "Fine. We'll go. But don't you think we're getting a little old for this?" He nodded to the dashboard on which the garish flyer lay.

"I think it looks fun," Julie replied, picking up the advertisement. A bloody, decapitated head with vacant eyes stared back at her as she read the caption aloud in a deep, dramatic voice: "'House of Screams. Get ready for a night of pure terror. We're *dying* to meet you.'"

When Zach did not respond, she said, "All right, it's not very original, but it's only twenty bucks per person, and the other ones I checked out were, like, at least twice as much. Trust me, it'll be fun." She smiled, her eyes pleading. A horror buff, she loved this sort of thing, whereas her boyfriend would have preferred to go park by the river and fool around.

"Whatever. But don't expect me to scream. And if it's lame, we're doing something else, okay?"

"Deal." Julie liked getting her way and was excited to leave town, away from the regular high school parties and football games. It was almost Halloween, after all; why not get into the spirit of things?

***

They pulled into a long, gravel driveway thirty minutes later. The disembodied voice of the GPS announced, "You have reached your destination."

Zach furrowed his brow. "Are you *sure* this is where we're supposed to go? Shouldn't there be a sign or something? I'd just feel better if I could get a signal on my phone and use my Maps app. The GPS on my car is old."

Pursing her lips, Julie said, "This *has* to be it. This is the only place around." She waved her arms to indicate the miles of Pennsylvania farmland surrounding them.

On the cool, crisp October day, with the setting sun illuminating the red and gold leaves falling upon rolling green hills, Julie felt a frisson of excitement to embark upon such a festive and spooky activity. "Look," she said, pointing out the goose bumps on her arm, "I'm scared already."

"That makes one of us," Zach muttered as he parked his ancient Ford and turned off the engine.

The couple got out of the car, stretching their limbs after the trip. "Are we the only ones here? Shouldn't there be other cars?" Zach asked.

Julie checked her phone again to see if Andrea had texted, but, like Zach, she didn't have cell reception this far out in the country. "Or maybe we're supposed to park near that huge barn over there? And I can't say I'm surprised that we beat Bobby and Andrea. She always takes *forever* to get ready. Like she needs to look all gorgeous to impress the guys dressed up as killer clowns?"

Julie felt annoyed by the familiar antics of the girl she didn't really care for that much, but the foursome spent considerable time together since Bobby and Zach were best friends. "We're here, so let's go. It's cold and I don't feel like waiting around. They can catch up with us inside, I guess. That must be the place."

The farmhouse, a slanted structure, gave the impression of abandonment, with several broken windows and rotting boards. Likewise, the surrounding grounds, despite the lush autumnal colors, appeared unkempt and in need of work, the grass long and dry.

"It *looks* like a haunted house, anyway," Zach said. "I wonder if they just found an old place or did stuff to make it look that way."

"It's probably special effects. It wouldn't pass the inspection if they used a real place. You know, safety hazards." Julie had no idea whether or not haunted house attractions needed any sort of government regulation, but she figured Zach would feel better if the place at least *sounded* like a legit attraction.

"Right. Let's get this over with." Zach scanned the area once more for the familiar green boat of Bobby's rusty Chevy Malibu in case it was somehow camouflaged behind one of the many skinny trees. "Let's give this place some much needed business."

Their sneakers crunched in the gravel as they walked, the only sound in the silence. Julie rubbed her hands together to stay warm.

"Where are the people who work here?" Zach asked. "You'd think they'd be up our butts by now trying to get our money. We're, like, their only customers."

Julie smiled, moving her eyebrows up and down. "I bet it's all part of their thing. You know, to make it seem real. They want us to think we're really about to go into a haunted house."

"If you ask me, this place needs better marketing. People probably get lost on their way here all the time, especially since they don't even have a sign. How do they get any business, anyway?"

"I don't know, Zach. Let's just get inside." Julie's tone was short. She had expected a carnival atmosphere; she'd been to "haunted" houses before with long lines, cotton candy stands, and the ever-present screeching of thirteen-year-old girls. Something didn't feel right about this place. Where *was* everyone?

"Where's the ticket booth?" Julie said, now that they had reached the door. "Do we just go inside? I don't know what to make of this. Do you think it's closed or something? Maybe that's why it's empty."

"They wouldn't send out the flyers if they weren't open. It costs money, and it looks like this place can use some, since no one's here." Zach stared into Julie's eyes, sensing her uneasiness. "I'm sure there's a zombie or something ready to collect our cash when we go inside."

As he twisted the knob, the door opened with a loud creak.

"Oh, that smell is awful!" Julie said in a small, strained voice as the odor of something rotten assaulted their nostrils.

His eyes tearing, Zach nodded, keeping his voice low, as if he were in a library. "You can buy these sprays to smell like stuff. I saw it on TV. That's *foul*."

They stepped forward, waiting to be surprised by the haunted house workers. "Ugh! It's sticky!" Leaning on Zach for support, Julie picked up her foot to see what she had stepped in, but the room's only light was the twilight glow through a hole in the ceiling. "Gross. I don't like that. It's like going to that five-dollar movie theater in town, that nasty one."

"I think it's supposed to be blood," Zach whispered. "Pretty freaky, I guess, but now we're gonna track that into my car."

"What's that sound?" Julie asked, not really caring about whether or not they would further besmirch Zach's beast of a vehicle. She cocked her head to the side to listen.

Now Zach was the one repulsed as he heard the buzzing. "It's flies." Sure enough, as their eyes adjusted, they could see the shapes of what must have been hundreds of the dirty little insects flying around in circles and landing back in the residue of the floor.

He batted the flies away. "Let's get out of here. I'm not even scared; I just feel like I could puke."

"Okay," Julie agreed, as her stomach was beginning to feel queasy; the pizza she had eaten a couple of hours earlier threatened to reappear. She turned back to the door and twisted the knob. "I can't open it."

"Lemme try." Zach pushed his girlfriend aside and struggled in vain. "It's locked somehow! Who could've locked it? We haven't even *seen* anyone."

"Maybe we have to get all the way *through* the house," Julie said, her voice panicked, shooing the flies away.

"No way," Zach said. "I'll break down the door if I have to." He kicked at the door again and again to no avail. "What the hell? This thing is solid. I can't knock it down. We have to find another way out!"

They trudged through the congealing puddles. "I think we're in some sort of kitchen," Zach whispered. In the dim lighting, they could make out a long wooden table with a ceramic bowl of what had once been fruit but was now only a fuzzy, gelatinous mass. The flies hovered in a black cloud over the rot. The table was bare except for this and one other object: a meat cleaver.

"Keep walking," Julie said, shaking, her voice barely audible. "Let's get out of here."

"It's thicker now," Zach said in a calm voice, referring to the substance on the floor. It was more of an effort to raise and lower their feet each time, but they wanted to get out, *had* to get out, back to the safety of their normal, comfortable world. "There's something—"

He stopped when his eyes rested upon the object blocking his way, a large, solid item. It looked like a pretty realistic prop, one made of rank, decomposing flesh. Zach opened his mouth to scream, but no sound emerged.

And then they heard the footsteps, slow and measured, along with the scrape of metal across wood as their pursuer located his weapon.

Zach and Julie registered the grizzled man in front of them. He was filthy, with long, tangled hair and torn clothing. He smiled, a demented grin.

"Welcome," he said. "I'd tell the wife to fix you a lemonade, but you can see she's not up to the task." He gestured to the dead, mutilated carcass on the floor. He fingered his weapon as if to test its sharpness.

"Look," Zach said. "We've changed our minds. We don't want to go through this haunted house. But don't worry! We'll still give you the forty dollars. We just want to leave. My girlfriend isn't feeling very well."

"Please, just let us leave," Julie managed, voice trembling. "We won't tell anyone."

The man coughed out a laugh. "Ha! Not sure why you two showed up, all the way out in the boonies, but you'll have to stay a while. A long while. Forever, in fact."

Lunging forward with his meat cleaver, the killer brought the weapon down forcefully, slicing through Zach's shoulder. Zach screamed but seemed in shock, as though he couldn't comprehend what had just happened. He was frozen in place as his arm fell to the floor. Blood spurted and splashed over Julie.

Her mouth contorting in horror, Julie ran blindly through the darkened, unfamiliar house. She didn't hear anything more from Zach, which terrified her further, but she had to try to save herself. There was nothing she could do for her boyfriend anymore.

Julie banged into a wall that she didn't see and changed course to enter another room. She searched frantically for some way out, or, at the very least, a place to hide.

Was that a back door? She lunged toward it only to be stopped mid-stride by the cleaver chopping into her chest.

***

"Where *are* they?" Andrea checked her phone for about the thirtieth time in two minutes. 7:30, and still no texts back. "This is sooooo annoying. How long do they think we're gonna wait for them? Didn't you tell them seven o'clock?"

Bobby said, "Let's just wait a couple minutes longer." It wasn't like Zach to be late, but maybe he had a flat or something. Bobby watched the line to the admission stand get longer and longer. *Man, this place is making a killing tonight*, he thought.

"We're gonna be waiting an hour if we don't get in line *now!*" Andrea's nagging voice sounded shrill even over the roar of the hundreds of customers eager to enter House of Screams, a popular "haunted house" attraction. The sweet odors of kettle corn and funnel cake permeated the air along with the rich, earthy smells of the farmland.

"Maybe they got lost," Bobby said. But the huge, flashing sign with the zombie head announced to everyone for at least a mile around where they could find the attraction. How could they miss it?

Andrea gave Bobby a long look. "All right," he said. "I guess we'll catch up with them later."

But no one would ever see Zach or Julie again. Their corpses would rot away in the small, remote farmhouse, where the farmer would eventually succumb to his own madness and join his victims in death and decay.

Zach and Julie would miss the cheap thrills their friends would enjoy, but thanks to an outdated GPS system and the unluckiness of walking into a murder scene, they had found their own House of Screams.

WINTER

NOT A CAT GUY

Hey, man. Yeah, I'll have another. Got a minute? There's something I need to get off my chest if you're willing to listen. Thanks.

So I start dating this woman, you know? Not a girl but a real woman—hot, smart, total wife material. I'm in my thirties now, so I need to be done with those party girls. I want someone to do real grownup shit with, like go to my nephew's birthday party or dinner at the boss's house. A *woman*. And then I meet Amber through a friend of a friend, and I figure she could be the one.

Things are going great for a while, slow, but whatever. She's been married before, but then her husband died like a year before I met her. That's how I got lucky and scooped her up, this chick totally out of my league—it turns out she was just putting herself back out there. Probably coulda gotten a better looking and more successful dude than me if she waited longer! She wasn't even on the apps yet.

Man, Amber's the real deal, like the first woman I dated who has opinions on stuff that matters, like politics and human rights and shit. She's just herself, you know? Unashamed to admit she enjoys reality TV and doesn't like watching sports or going to museums—she says she works all the time and is gonna do whatever she wants when it's *her* time. She says life's too short to do only what other people tell you.

We go through our honeymoon getting-to-know-you phase and hash some shit out. She says she's afraid to let her guard down around me after being epically wounded by her husband's death, and I make the mistake of saying I don't mind damaged goods, trying to keep it light, but that does *not* go over well, more like a fart at a funeral. At that point, I haven't been to her house yet, and that all comes out. We'd been together a couple of months by then, but we'd always gone to my place.

But we're solid, so we both apologize for what we said. Before I know it, she invites me over for this romantic dinner. And that's the night I meet *him*.

Amber mentioned she had a cat, and I'm not a cat guy, but I don't really care one way or the other. He's a rescue, an older kitten she adopted from the local shelter like six months before we met. No big deal to me since I'm not allergic; I'd just rather hang with a dog.

So, the night of, I put her address in my phone and drive like half an hour from my place to this fancy-ass neighborhood, a tree-lined cul-de-sac with brick and stone houses and a big sign announcing the swanky place, Thistle Grove. And I'm thinking that thistles are weeds, but still, it's the whole nine. And I'm feeling a little insecure if you wanna know the truth, with me living in a townhouse and the kind of restaurants I've been taking her to, but whatever. I'm here to check out my girlfriend's digs. I thought I was all suave buying her flowers—just a bouquet of daisies I picked up while getting some wine for dinner at the grocery store—and then I realize that both the flowers and wine are cheap and tacky, but I suck up my pride and head up the elaborate hardscaped walkway.

Amber swings the door open before I even reach it, wearing a low-cut black dress that I'm already imagining curled up on the floor of her no-doubt glamourous bedroom. She puts her arms around me even though mine are full and plants a soft, wet kiss on my lips, so I let go of my doubts and walk right on in.

Amber's giving me a tour of her place, and I'm feeling like a total schmuck when she pulls out this crystal vase for my pathetic flowers which look like crap in her tasteful foyer—probably foy-yay or whatever. And I'm wondering if I'm good enough for her, but then I know I'm not by the time we make it to the dining room where there's this huge-ass wooden table that I know isn't from Ikea or Target like pretty much all my furniture, and it's all laid out with dinner plates and real cloth napkins like it's a wedding or at least a prom or something, and the smell is incredible like I died and went to heaven, but then that starts me thinking about her dead husband, the only reason I'm here in the first place.

Not gonna lie—I kinda peeked around for his picture when I was oohing and aahing over all the art and hardwood floors and shit, and I don't wanna be obvious, like how can I be jealous of a dead man when I'm the one who's gonna take Amber to bed that night? And I think I see a picture of her in a white dress with some dude, but it's not like a rule that she has to put photos of her dead husband away just 'cause her new boyfriend's over.

So I'm busy trying to act normal and appreciative of her effort, since I know Amber doesn't like to cook but she's still made this awesome fettuccine alfredo and garlic bread anyway, and now I'm thinking I look like a clown slurping noodles off this fancy silverware, so I tell her about the (cheap) wine being from Chile and how my buddy Derek and his wife went on a trip there and no one ever heard from them again even though both sets of their parents went down there and launched a GoFundMe. I even donated a couple hundred bucks. I miss that guy. And I find myself getting upset talking about it, wondering what happened, but then Amber's slender fingers are stroking my shoulder, making me feel better.

But that's when *he* comes sauntering in and jumps right up on the dining room table. Amber starts shooing him away and apologizing, and I'm kinda skeeved out that a cat's sitting right by the garlic bread after he might've just been messing around in his litter box, but I don't wanna be difficult when she's been so sweet and gone to all this trouble for me. I say it's fine, and the fucking cat stays there, his ass right on the table, and glares at me with these green eyes.

Amber's like, "This is my baby, Jacques." I hate when people call their pets their babies or their fur babies—it's a cat or a dog, not a baby. She gets into this whole thing about the darkness she felt after her husband died, but then she adopted the cat and he helped her find joy again.

Trying to be a good guy and thankful that this furball perked her up, I go ahead and give the little dude a pet. I figure that he helped get her ready to meet me, so I should be grateful. But the asshole swerves his head around like in *The Exorcist* and sinks his fangs into the meat of my hand. I don't wanna act like a wuss or harm him, but he does *not* let go, and it hurts like hell.

Amber starts freaking out and I'm trying not to scream or flail him around, but then Amber finally pulls him off me, and I'm dripping blood straight into my pasta. The cat runs out of the room after fixing me with this death stare.

Amber's all over it, running around with bandages and hydrogen peroxide, and I try to act chill but that fucker was surprisingly strong, and the punctures look and feel deep. Not to mention he has a mouth full of bacteria, so I'm picturing my hand swelling up with green pus and needing to get amputated.

But then I'm bandaged and cared for, and we're in the bedroom with our wine, and Amber feels so bad that she's giving me extra attention, rubbing my shoulders and taking off that dress and kissing my neck, and I kinda feel like my injury might have been worth it.

Afterward, we're nodding off in her big, magnificent bed. But then I jolt awake to this scratching sound at the door—really irritating, like fingernails on a chalkboard. In the moonlight streaming through the window, I see that fucker Jacques sneak into the bedroom. He jumps up on the bed and curls right up on Amber's chest like he didn't go all cat-Cujo on me! She's sound asleep by now and doesn't even register him, but I'm not messing around. I pull myself all the way to the edge of the king bed putting as much distance between us as possible, and I swear he smiles at me, but not a nice smile like he wants to be friends, more like he's laughing at me. But I somehow go back to sleep anyway, even though I'm a little nervous, to be honest.

When I wake up in the morning, before I even open my eyes, I'm aware of being watched and of a pressure on my chest. Sure enough, that bastard's sitting right on top of me, staring into my eyeballs like he's figuring out how to end me.

Amber's awake, too, smiling at us. "I think he's sorry," she says, giving him a pat.

This tremendous growl starts inside of the cat, and I'm waiting for him to lash out, waiting for new pain, for his claws to slash me across my face. My wounded hand stings in sympathy for whatever comes next.

"Relax, Jason, he's purring," she says, sensing my discomfort. "Pet him."

As much as I don't trust him, I don't like disappointing Amber, so I do, hoping Jacques doesn't want to upset her, either. And, I have to admit, that black fur is soft and silky under the fingers of my good hand, and he *is* kind of cute, but I won't forget what he did to me. He gives me this long, slow blink like he's trying to tell me something, but I don't speak cat, and Amber's gushing away.

Before I know it, she's confessing her love for me and asking do I wanna move in.

We push the cat out of the way, him with a departing hiss directed at me even though I was just being nice to the little fella, and I swear that creep watches us the whole time we make love, but I look at Amber and remind myself how lucky I am. Amber leaves when we're done to take a shower, and soon Jacques jumps back on the bed, greeting me with another hiss and squinting his eyes like he wants to rip the skin off my face. I scowl back, but Amber's walking back into the bedroom with a towel on her head, and the cat slinks away.

Fast forward a month, and my townhouse is on the market and I'm moving my shit into Amber's place, giving away or taking all my chintzy furniture to Goodwill since it's not gonna fit in with her classy stuff. The cat's still screwing with me whenever Amber's not looking—growling and swiping at me, throwing up in my shoes, I shit you not—but it's like we have a truce whenever Amber's around. He doesn't mess with me and I don't mess with him, not that I really do anyway. He's just a cat, but I glare at him and tell him to fuck off occasionally.

And then Amber goes on this business trip for a few days—she works at Samson, Green, & Associates, you ever heard of them? It's just the cat and me in her huge freaking house, and I'm in charge of feeding him and cleaning the litter box and stuff, which feels weird since the cat and I don't even get along, but she said she needs to be able to trust me to take care of him. I briefly consider hiring the teenage boy next door to do it, but I chicken out imagining Amber upset with me if she finds out.

So she's gone and I'm basically the cat's bitch now, feeding him this fancy gourmet food in his crystal dish like he's the king of cats, and Amber wants me to send a picture every day so she knows he's okay. I play along, trying to catch him sleeping so he doesn't hassle me, but we give each other a wide berth, more or less. He knows he needs me to give him food, and I know I need to be nice so Amber doesn't heave me to the curb.

But I swear he's still playing mind games with me. He wakes me up wailing at like five a.m. the first morning when he knows I'll be up for work in an hour anyway, and I go down to the living room to see what's the matter, like if he caught a mouse or something. He shuts up when I get there, so I turn on the light, not sure what to expect, and I see he's knocked down a picture frame—

broke the glass and everything. I put on some shoes so I don't cut my feet, and I pick up the picture, and it's actually the wedding picture, Amber's wedding to her first husband, Greg.

Call it my ego, but I never took a good look at it, didn't really want to act like he'd existed. But I'm forced to look now, my eyes still adjusting to the light, and that's when I see that this homeboy Greg has jet black hair and these light green eyes glowing out from the picture. And as I'm looking at this picture of the dead man who used to live here, this guy Amber loved before she even knew I existed, the cat starts making this weird noise, this chirping sound. I don't know what to make of it, so I replace the picture, clean up the glass, and go back to bed, but I can't sleep. I keep thinking about Greg, wondering what he was like and thinking how, if he'd lived, I wouldn't be with Amber. And I feel kinda shitty for admitting this, but I'm glad he died.

Amber comes home the next day, and I have to tell her about Jacques knocking down and breaking the glass, and I feel weird since we never really talk about her ex.

"He's not my ex, he died," she reminds me, and I'm chastened and shamed, and I don't know if she thinks *I'm* the one who knocked it over instead of the cat, and maybe was he trying to get me in trouble?

But now that we're kinda talking about the not-ex-husband, it's like the ice is broken around the subject, and she brings him up more and more, like *Greg* used to do this and *Greg* liked that, and I'm feeling less and less adequate since this guy was handsome and basically a genius theology professor at Blackthorn University, not to mention loaded, like *old money* money, and I'm just an average-looking dude from Jersey who sells insurance. And she asks me to help her take some of his old stuff to Goodwill—he had all these books his family doesn't want and Amber doesn't want, either.

So I'm already living in the house this guy's money bought and shtupping his wife, so I figure I might as well go through his books to see if I can make sense of them. I'd like to think I'm not a total dumbass, but I can't make heads or tails of them, all these religious textbooks. But I see this one that looks interesting, like almost homemade, with this weird leather cover, no title or author on it, and the inside's all crinkly and old with faded writing that looks handwritten. No way it came from a regular bookstore or publisher. And—get this—it's all about reincarnation. And I know that fits in with his research or whatever, but it's also about how you can *make* yourself come back after you die.

Most of it's over my head, and my hands feel tingly from touching it, like it's enchanted with black magic, so I get kinda spooked and make sure it's in the first box to head out of the house.

And that's when I think back to Greg's picture from their wedding, how he had black hair and green eyes, and I'm thinking about all this as I look up and see the fucking cat staring at me with this smug look on his face.

I know it's crazy, but it all starts coming together, and I think back to how long ago Greg died and when Amber got the cat, and how old the cat was when she got him and also how he hates me even though I've been feeding him and cleaning up after him, so I stare him right in the face and ask him if he's Greg.

I'm half expecting him to open his mouth and talk to me, but he just lifts up his leg and starts cleaning himself, which I'm pretty sure means *fuck you* in cat language.

So I start doing some deep diving on the internet, looking up stuff about Greg and how he died, which I never asked Amber about 'cause I wanted to respect her privacy and what she shared with her husband, but if the husband's actually Jacques then I need to be able to protect myself. I find out Greg had leukemia, but I also find this picture of him about a year before he died at this temple in India somewhere, and I think that's where he got that book and plotted coming back as Jacques.

And Jacques knows I'm on to him, and I start wondering what he's going to do to me, if he's going to try to get rid of me somehow, so I start acting extra careful, making sure he can't get me into trouble somehow. But he's smart—you need to be in school forever to get a PhD, you know? And I don't know how much he retained from his life as a man, but Jacques definitely has my number by this time.

Then I have this crazy dream one night—at least I think it's a dream. Jacques is speaking to me in what I know is Greg's voice since I found some clips of him online from academic conferences where he gave presentations, and he's telling me that Amber is his and he's gonna find a way to get rid of me, and I know this shouldn't be scary since it's more like a Disney movie with a fucking talking cat, but I wake up in a cold sweat with my heart pounding out of my chest. And the cat's staring at me like it all really happened, and maybe it did.

I don't say anything to Amber through any of this, just keep acting like everything's fine and she has a perfectly normal asshole of a cat versus a dead husband reincarnated as a cat. I know I'd sound crazy, and she wouldn't like that I'm snooping around trying to find things out about Greg and looking at all the articles he wrote and listening to some of his recorded lectures and stuff.

But then one day I'm chilling watching the game and she comes home from work, and, before she even gives me a kiss, she's calling for her precious little Jacques, so I go back to watching TV. I don't even realize how much time has passed until she's standing in front of me screaming and crying, and I'm just like, "What?"

She says I left the back door open and Jacques is gone, like, out of the house gone, and that he could be lying dead on the side of the road somewhere because he's not an outside cat and doesn't know how crossing the street works. And part of me thinks how peaceful it would be without Jacques, but I know not to say that just like I know I didn't leave the door open. I know *he* did it to frame me.

Three days. Three days Amber's sobbing every night, missing him, giving me the cold shoulder. I'm trying to do all the good boyfriend stuff—put up flyers, you know, contact rescue centers. Somebody calls us and we go to meet them, but it's some other black cat. I would've been happy to take any other cat home and just pretend it's Jacques, so I even try to make her think it's him, but she gets all pissed off like how could I possibly think this scraggly thing is her sweet baby, and I'm hoping this dude isn't also a man reincarnated, 'cause it's pretty harsh to say that about him when he's just a poor stray cat with no one to love him.

So Jacques is still gone, and I try to cheer Amber up, bring her Starbucks and stuff, give her a foot massage, the whole nine, but she's livid with me even though I'm innocent. And we're sitting in the living room, me finally getting pissed off that she's blaming me, her crying and snotting everywhere, and then we hear this scratch at the door.

So I get up to open the door, and there's that cocky little bastard, looking roughed up and dirty, and he just runs into the house and launches himself onto her lap.

It's this big tearful reunion between them, so I go over thinking I'll get back into Amber's good graces. I go to pet Jacques and he lunges at me, scratching my hand.

But Amber doesn't fawn all over me like when Jacques bit me that first time I came over. She's all like, "I knew it. I knew you didn't like him! I knew you let him out!" She's up on her feet, her face all scrunched up and red, tears and mucus streaking her face, shouting, cursing at me, and I'm pretty much in shock since I still didn't even do anything to the damn cat, but I look over and see the cat laughing at me.

I try to reason with her, try to make her see it was Jacques trying to come between us, and I spill the beans about Greg and how he found out how to come back to her. She looks at me like I'm a lunatic, so I give her all my proof, and she goes all still before telling me we're done.

She gives me to the end of that week to move out. So that's that, and Jacques/Greg gets the girl.

Yeah, yeah, I know you have other customers, but I'm your best one, right? And can I get one more beer, man? Just trying to take the edge off before I head home to my shitty new apartment where I'm sleeping on a futon since I sold my place and got rid of my furniture. Thanks, man. That fucking cat.

CHRISTMAS MARKET MASSACRE

The enormous glittering tree towers over the abandoned stalls of Christkindli Markt.

With no time for the shopkeepers to lock up their wares in the pandemonium, cheerful-looking wooden Samichlauses and wide-eyed snowmen are left to stare out from their shelters at the desolation.

Sweet and savory aromas of decadent food mingle with the pungent reek spilling from the victims' mouths. Littering the ground, along with the crumpled paper cups from which the tainted Glühwein puddles like blood, lay the corpses of the fallen.

Some have succumbed to the poison while others were trampled to death as the former merry makers fled the catastrophe, leaving the unlucky to perish behind them.

Silken tresses of blonde hair tumble out of a winter hat. The young American woman no longer feels the cold of the linoleum floor beneath her. Her glassy eyes remain open, forever sightless.

***

12 hours earlier

Stacey slowly opens her sleep-encrusted eyes.

Damn. She's ashamed to admit it, but she can't quite remember getting back to the hotel last night. She glances across the room to see Amanda, her mouth open in slumber. A raucous snore escapes from between her lips.

Thank goodness. Things could have been so much worse. They're in a foreign country—they can't mess around like this. *Anything* could have happened, and they're lucky to be waking up in their own hotel room, safe.

Getting trashed every night of winter break wasn't the plan when the roommates embarked on this weeklong European adventure, but it has become the reality. It's been back-to-back nights of biergartens and bars, first in Munich and now in Zurich. Stacey rushes to the bathroom to relieve her stomach, hurling her guts into the abyss.

***

"I can't believe how wasted you got," Amanda says. "Your retching actually woke me up."

"Sorry," Stacey replies, her throat sore and raw. The taste of hot, rancid bile hasn't left her mouth even after toothpaste and mouthwash. "I don't think we should have drunk those shots."

"Hey, you didn't have to say yes when that Belgian guy offered to buy them. He was hitting on me, anyway. It's just crazy that I can handle more liquor than you." Amanda's vision rakes over Stacey's considerably larger frame.

Stacey crosses her arms, self-conscious. It's not the first time Amanda's referenced their dissimilar sizes, or their different financial statuses, for that matter. With all the hours she spends as an office worker in the chemistry department when she's not in class or completing homework, she hasn't gotten to the gym as much as she would have liked. A senior now, she's yet to shed that cursed freshman fifteen. And she's been working more hours than usual to help pay for this trip, an expense that Amanda had casually placed on her credit card for her parents to pay.

"Maybe we should eat," Amanda suggests.

Stacey feels empty. A nice, greasy plate of bacon and eggs might help.

***

Heading to the small continental spread set up in the lobby, Stacey grabs a croissant, avoiding the mysterious morning cold cuts and hard-boiled eggs. Her stomach lurches as her eyes find the bottles of champagne near the orange juice.

"Hair of the dog?" Amanda asks, smirking. "You sure liked your booze *last* night."

Stacey sticks to juice and coffee.

***

Having completed their requisite daily cultural activity, a trip to the art museum at which they found Insta-worthy photo ops that are also tame enough to text home to their parents, they're back in a bar. It's pretty rundown with garish fluorescent lighting and wooden furniture that looks like someone's grandmother's dining room set. Still, the proximity to the museum makes it ideal for a quick refueling station before they head back to the hotel to get ready for tonight.

Amanda sets down two pints of beer on the plastic checkered tablecloth. "The bartender said we should go to the Christmas market later. Should we?"

Stacey takes a big gulp. Now that her stomach has finally settled, the pilsner goes down in a cool, refreshing swallow. "Of course we should go! It's a whole thing, these Christmas markets. I can't believe I forgot! I learned about this when I researched the trip in the summer!"

Amanda glances back at the bartender. "He's cute, but I don't even know if he was hitting on me or even planning on going. I don't wanna get stuck at some place for old people and families if it means we'll miss out on better night life. A month from now we'll be back in classes and hanging at keg parties with boring frat boys, so I want to soak up as much *real* culture as I can while we're here."

Stacey bites back her comment as she often does. Arguing with Amanda about what constitutes culture won't get her anywhere—her best bet is a compromise. She's already on her phone, looking up details. "Look, it's only open until 10:00 tonight, and you know that the clubs will be open way after that. Can we just please check it out? Please?"

"Sure, my merry little elf. But *you're* buying *me* a shot tonight." They clink glasses.

***

The girls walk through the open doors of the train station into the enormous indoor marketplace. "Wow," Stacey says, unable to help herself. "It's beautiful, like a Christmas fairy tale."

A massive, dazzling chandelier hangs from the center of the ceiling, its jellyfish-like tentacles cascading down in a display of multi-colored lights over the festive scene below.

More than a hundred stalls are set up, selling all kinds of items: ornaments, scarves, hats, figurines, watches, and toys. Food is plentiful: sausage sandwiches, stews, potato pancakes, steak rolls, pastries, nuts, and chocolates.

White fairy lights, nestled in evergreen boughs affixed to the rooftops, sparkle as Christmas carols play from speakers over the muffled laughs and roars of the revelers.

The piece-de-resistance, though, is the fifty-foot high Christmas tree dripping with thousands of crystal icicles and snowflakes, standing tall behind protective glass shields and commanding the viewer to behold its majesty.

"The Rockefeller tree is way bigger." Amanda waves her hand dismissively. "Let's find some drinks."

Stacey inhales a delectable scent, but she knows she needs to keep Amanda happy. Drinks first, then dinner.

Amanda's already sizing up the options. "What's up with all the coffee cups stacked everywhere?"

"Maybe it's booze? Those people definitely look drunk." Stacey points to a young, ruddy-faced couple practically falling out of their seats.

"Let's ask." She's heading over, her boots clacking on the floor, before Stacey can suggest an alternative. "Hi. My friend and I want to know what you're drinking?"

"It's Glühwein," the man tells her in accented English, not even looking at Stacey. "Delicious."

"Blue wine?" Amanda asks, peering into his cup far too closely. "It looks red."

"No, Glühwein. You know, mulled wine? Hot spiced wine. We drink it for Christmas. Would you like to try?" He offers his cup.

"No thanks," Stacy says, pulling her friend away. The man points them to the stall where he got it.

There's a bit of a line, and Amanda taps her feet, anxious to get her drink on. Stacey doesn't mind the wait, happy to watch the bartenders fill cup after cup, pausing only to collect the Swiss francs. Normally, on a Thursday night over winter break, Stacey would be hanging out in the basement of a friend from high school, maybe drinking a Bud Light. Instead, she's at a Zurich Christmas market, about to indulge in a local tradition! She's hardly ever even drunk wine before, and what she tried came from a box.

They're finally up. "Zwei Glühweins, danke," Stacey says, remembering her high school German enough for a halfway decent pronunciation.

The bartender sniffs and corrects her anyway. A girl about their age who wears only a low-cut tee shirt despite the cold of the train station, she turns to one of the two enormous urns behind her and flips the tap. Stacey watches in delight as the steaming liquid fills each paper cup.

She takes just a moment to enjoy the warmth under her bare fingers and breathe in the spicy aroma.

"Prost!" Amanda uses her favorite new vocab, the German word for "cheers," tapping her cup to her roommate's and taking a big sip. "Damn, that's hot!"

"I don't think we're supposed to chug it!" Stacey takes her first taste slowly, savoring this moment drinking Glühwein at the Christkindli Markt in Zurich. Truly, this is a Christmas like no other, doing something she had never dreamed possible in this magical place with more festivities in store. She smiles as the sweet, warm liquid trickles down her throat, making her feel like she's glowing inside. "Let's go sit where we can see the big tree and enjoy our drinks."

"Refill first? We're right here." She points to the steadily-growing line already snaking around them. "Then we'll sit. I promise. It doesn't seem like this alcohol content is too high, and I'd like to get a buzz going before we chill."

Stacey shrugs. She's promised herself to take it easy tonight, but Amanda can do what she likes. She always does, anyway.

***

About an hour or so later, the girls sit in companionable silence taking in their surroundings. Stacey's polished off a bratwurst and some fancy Swiss chocolates; Amanda says she's not hungry but has had a couple more cups of Glühwein.

"I wonder if I can get this at home?" she mumbles. "This is amazing." Flushed from the mulled wine, Amanda unzips her Northface jacket.

Maybe they won't make it out to the club that night, after all.

***

There's only one bartender left at the Glühwein stand. "I will be ready to serve in five minutes!" she calls in English after saying probably the same thing in German. Based on the increased rowdiness of the crowd, most people have indulged quite a bit already, and they're waiting for the new batch to heat up.

Amanda's swaying a bit on her feet—she drank far too fast, and the beer from earlier plus a glass of champagne at the hotel weren't helping matters. "Last one. Then we'll go to the club."

"Sure." Stacey's satiated with food and drink and would prefer to put on her flannel jammies. But she'll hang here with Amanda. It's what friends do.

***

A shrill scream reverberates through the train station. "Hilfe! Mein Ehemann!"

Stacey and Amanda sit at a table near the Christmas tree, empty cups before them. Despite how much Amanda had already consumed, Stacey didn't protest when Amanda finished her own Glühwein and moved on to hers.

Stacey whips her head around, searching for the source of the scream.

Not too far away, chaos unfolds. An older woman hovers over her husband, who is convulsing on the floor. Nearby, another shriek breaks out, and another.

Amanda, slumped in her chair, attempts to right herself, to sit up properly and find the source of the drama. Instead, she crashes to the floor.

"Amanda?" Stacey's cries add to the cacophony. She holds her roommate's hand as Amanda's taut, trim body seizes and her blonde head hits the floor again and again.

She dials 911. But that's not the emergency number in Switzerland.

It's too late anyway. Stacey sees the light flee from her roommate's eyes, watches her take her last slow, shallow breaths. She allows herself to be washed away with the tide as the mass exodus begins, sailing along with the bodies rather than risking being pulled under.

***

When the Swiss police investigate, after several false starts, they finally find the source weeks later: cyanide in that last batch of Glühwein.

No one took any notice when the tall, slightly overweight friend of the prettier girl abandoned the line for a few moments. Impatient with the wait for their next drink, no one noticed the activity around the back of the stall.

The police will never find the culprit, the person responsible for twelve lost lives.

How could they? She's already back in Pennsylvania, starting her last semester before she graduates with her bachelor's degree in chemistry.

HUNGRY CHRISTMAS

"I *told* you we should have waited until after the storm," Cole said, brow furrowed in consternation as he peered through the windshield. Even with the wipers on full speed, he couldn't keep his field of vision clear; the frost encroached as the minutes ticked by. From the shrinking porthole, the road stretched out before them, a narrowing black snake, the earlier dusting of snow transforming into a heavy, white blanket devouring the pavement.

Henry shivered, though the heater was cranked on full blast, and his linebacker's build left him with plenty of padding, unlike the lean quarterback in the driver's seat. Always defending himself to his bossy and complaining roommate, teammate, and longtime friend, sometimes Henry felt tired. "I just wanted to see my mom, you know? Help her wrap the presents for my little bro."

Though the other guys in the dorm had headed home right after finals, Cole and Henry stayed a week later—a chance for the freshmen on the Blackthorn University football team to earn their stripes. It was fine, really; Henry liked having access to a nearly empty gym, and they'd helped set up a makeshift football camp for the local elementary school kids. But now it was nearly Christmas, and it had been brutal, balancing classes and football all semester.

Henry needed the comforts of home and family. He yearned to gorge himself on homemade sugar cookies while watching Christmas movies in front of a fire. He could picture the tree with its multi-colored lights and all of the goofy ornaments from over the years, souvenirs from vacations and simple art projects he and his brother made in elementary school. Christmas at Henry's house sure wasn't fancy compared to Cole's family, with the decorations looking like they came straight out of a Pottery Barn catalogue, but he didn't want it any other way. Henry hadn't wanted to wait a single extra night to head home.

"Damn! I think the wipers froze!" Cole exclaimed, bringing Henry back to the present. The clear space on the window shrunk even more, and Cole's attempt to spray the windshield fluid was in vain. The liquid must have frozen.

Henry tried to help by turning up the defroster, but it was already on the highest setting. "Okay, we're the only car on the road. Just slow down and try to concentrate," he said, his voice tranquil while his heart raced. What if they crashed? What if the car wouldn't go any farther and they froze to death?

"I *am* concentrating. It's what I've *been* doing while you're just sitting there like a lard ass staring out the window."

Henry decided to give him a pass on his testiness; Cole was always ragging on Henry's weight, had been ever since they were kids. Cole, the rich, golden boy and straight A student; Henry, the fat kid without a dad who barely scraped by. Football brought them together and kept them that way, even though they didn't have that much in common.

"Okay, we're about to head up a slight hill," Henry said, his voice soft as he attempted to exude a sense of calm over his teammate. "Nice and steady. I'll turn the hazards on just in case anyone comes up behind us."

Cole slapped his hand away. "Stop touching my car! I just need to focus."

But attention wasn't the issue. For all the elegance of Cole's Lexus, it couldn't climb even this minor incline. The wheels started spinning, unable to grip the asphalt beneath the snow and ice, and the car stopped, unable to trudge any further.

Henry waited for Cole's tirade of profanity to stop. "Looks like we're stuck. Let's—"

"No shit, Sherlock! We just need some traction."

As Henry cracked his door, a gust of snow and ice crept into the car. "There's about six inches on the road by now. I don't think we'll be able to move."

More swearing and pushing the pedal to no avail. Finally understanding the hopelessness, Cole said, "Okay, let's call Triple A and get towed. We're what, like fifty miles away from home? My dad can come get us in his truck."

Henry nodded. "First we gotta get this car off the road so no one rams into us." With daylight fading fast, the black car would soon become shrouded in darkness, nearly invisible to another hapless driver, with only the hazards providing a sign of their existence.

Henry got out of the car, wishing for snow boots instead of his old Converses. Using his bulk to push the car from behind while Cole navigated the steering wheel, they eventually managed to reach the shoulder, or at least what they thought was the shoulder, since they couldn't see anything under the accumulating snow.

Climbing back in, Henry blew on his hands. He relished the heat just for a moment. "Turn off the car," he commanded. "We don't know how long we'll have to wait. And call your dad, and then we can figure out a tow truck."

Cole was already doing just that. "No!" he screamed, tossing his iPhone into the back seat. "No service! Are you kidding me? Try yours. Now."

"No service." The two most depressing words he could utter. They were, essentially, in the middle of nowhere—no nearby gas station or rest stop, no cell phone towers, no other *cars*. "I'm sure a plow will be by soon, and then we can clear out."

***

Two hours later, snow still falling, darkness fully descended, they got their wish.

Sort of.

They'd found some protein bars in the glove compartment and eaten those, and Henry added a hoodie he'd found in his backpack to his layers. He offered it to Cole, but Cole said it was ugly and smelled. It *was* kind of hideous, some cheap thing from Walmart, but freshly laundered.

Henry's gut panged from hunger as he imagined the hearty dinner waiting for him at home, maybe meatloaf or lasagna. Instead of listening to Cole's griping, he'd be laughing as his little brother told him about his latest pranks. But here he was, stuck in a car.

Still no service, though they kept checking. Every ten minutes or so, Cole turned on the car for a quick burst of heat and then turned it off to conserve gas. Even if a plow didn't come by until morning, they'd be okay as long as they warmed up every now and then.

And then came the glorious rumble of an approaching vehicle. Except for Cole's bellyaching and the haunting roar of wind around them, it had been entirely silent.

"It's a snow plow! Hallelujah!" Cranky old Cole just about clapped his hands in glee. "We're set! We—"

But his words were cut off, as the snow plow, practically racing on the seemingly abandoned road, clipped the Lexus hard enough to push it off the shoulder and into the ditch.

***

How many times did the car roll? How far did it fall? Henry didn't know. He had his seatbelt on when it happened, having refastened it after getting out of the car to pee earlier. His body sore where the heavy cloth dug in, he was otherwise unscathed.

"Cole? You alright, man?" he asked, after the vehicle shuddered to a stop, and right side up, at that.

But Cole was *not* alright. Flung into the back seat, he lay at an unnatural angle, his neck crooked and eyes open.

"Cole? Buddy? You okay?"

Silence. And then a loud wail erupted, filling the car. Henry realized that he was the one making the sound.

***

Hours later, and still no cell signal, not on his phone and not on Cole's. Henry knew not to turn on the car for warmth anymore, remembering from some Boy Scout meeting of long ago that the carbon monoxide would kill him if the car was blocked by snow, which it was. Not only did the plow ram the car off the road, but it pushed off a ton of snow, too, and now all Henry could see from the window was white. But it was insulating, that deadly snow, and he was warm enough in his layers that he figured he'd survive the night. He could see his breath, but it wasn't too bad.

Right, his breath. What about oxygen? Should he try to break a window and dig himself out? Was it better to risk suffocating in a car, trapped with a corpse, or should he risk exposure? Where would he go even if he *could* escape this cocoon? He'd freeze to death on the side of the road.

He tried to sleep, wanting to mentally escape his prison. Henry pictured himself home, in bed, with the quilt his mother made wrapped around him.

***

Wide awake and ice cold, Henry checked his phone. 6:03 a.m. Surely a rescue crew would be looking for them now. He imagined the relief on his mother's tearstained face when she'd finally get to see him, to hug him. And he pictured Cole's parents, devastated when they learned the news about their own son. Guiltily, he looked at Cole, whose eyes remained open but now cloudy. He remembered in second grade when Roxanne, the girl he liked, confided in him that Cole Sumner had the most gorgeous eyes she'd ever seen.

Not so pretty now.

***

More time passed, and Henry didn't know how much, since his phone had died and so had Cole's. He wished he wore a watch so he could know the time, but he wished lots of things. Here it was, Christmas Eve, and all he wanted from Santa was rescue.

But no one came.

From within the car, through the snow, he watched and waited as the sun came up and went down again.

He had a water bottle in his bag, and he drank it. He drank Cole's, too, and found another use for the empty bottle. Henry turned the car on—just for a moment—to roll down the window enough to check out how deeply he was buried. As the snow started flooding the car, he pressed the button again to furiously roll it back up. He turned off the car in defeat.

He'd wait for rescue. That was safest. They had to come for him soon.

***

Henry really wasn't a science guy—he didn't know the facts and couldn't even look anything up on his dead phone. The air felt okay. He *seemed* to have enough oxygen.

But he was *so* hungry.

Nearly six and a half feet tall with a barrel chest and thick arms and legs, Henry was huge, with an appetite nearly as enormous. He was a Double Whopper with cheese, large fries, and chocolate milkshake kind of a guy.

He didn't know if he'd ever gone for more than about twelve hours without food, and a big meal at that.

But all he'd had in the past day or so was a protein bar and some water. Henry remembered the last time he'd been home, nearly a month ago now, for Thanksgiving. He recalled biting into the tender, succulent turkey breast, savoring the sweet, tangy cranberry sauce, and inhaling the rich, gooey pumpkin pie.

He was so ravenous he started feeling lightheaded. Henry ate some snow that had fallen in when he opened the window. It tasted like nothing and failed to quench his hunger.

***

Morning again, Henry could tell from the lightened snow outside the windows. Christmas Day and no rescue. He wanted to sleep and escape from the confines of this car with his deceased companion. He wanted to fill his belly with food instead of sadness and despair. Where the hell were his rescuers?

***

By nightfall he was almost delirious from hunger. And that's when he started to wonder. How long could he survive here, with no food and only snow for moisture?

He remembered learning about the Donner Party, way back when in middle school. He remembered Cole saying they'd eat Henry first, since he was the fattest and could feed the rest of the class.

And he remembered his pocketknife, the one on his keychain. He opened the blade, testing the sharpness with his finger.

Henry reached into the backseat, to Cole.

Just act, don't think. It had worked for him in football, and it would have to work here.

He pulled the sleeve back from Cole's cold, dead arm, feeling for meat. Cole spent hours in the gym and had very little body fat, but Henry found a nice bit of flesh on the inner forearm, near the elbow.

As Henry sliced into his friend's tissue, the thick, lazy blood oozed but did not gush. Cole's eyes, sightless, continued to stare, to accuse.

Cole had said he'd eat *him*, hadn't he? Wouldn't Cole be doing this very thing if their roles were switched?

Henry pondered this as he bit into Cole's lifeless flesh. And despite his horror, despite his sorrow, he chewed and swallowed and cut again.

Henry ate his Christmas dinner and thought about turkey.

***

It was too late when the cops finally discovered the car, more than a week later, buried under the snow. At the urging of Henry's bereft mother, and going off the data from the last cell phone pings, they had continued to canvas the area.

The dogs found them. Barking, they dragged their handlers to the ditch. The cops dug through the snow to finally reveal Cole's battered black Lexus.

They were expecting two corpses, dead from injury or suffocation or hypothermia or dehydration, or some combination of those factors.

What they found were one and a half.

TOGETHER FOR CHRISTMAS

It should have been a cheery scene: the crackling fire over which hung stockings, and the Christmas tree trimmed with sentimental ornaments from over the years, homemade ones from the kids and souvenirs from their cross-country travels. But even the sparkling lights and rich pine scent could not detract from what was missing.

Vera. It just wasn't Christmas without her.

Jacob sighed. He had tried so hard over the past six months to put on a brave front for his grown-up sons, each of whom had invited him to spend Christmas with them. "I'll be fine," he assured them. "I'll put out all your mother's decorations at home. It's what she would want."

He was wrong, and he knew it. Vera wouldn't have wanted him moping about, drinking mulled wine alone on Christmas Eve when he could have been celebrating with his remaining family. Sure, Hank had the twins to deal with now, but maybe he and his wife would have liked Jacob's help. Maybe they would've enjoyed his company, not to mention his cooking skills. He made a mean steak that everyone loved. And then there was Caleb, such a good man who appreciated the wisdom and humor of his dear old dad. He and his boyfriend had made a convincing argument to come with them to a cabin in Tahoe for the holiday, a trip that sounded filled with fun and adventure.

Jacob couldn't do it. He knew the boys loved him and worried about him, but he didn't want to intrude on their holiday, nor did he want to leave his town or his house. Why deal with the stress of travel?

For forty years, he had spent Christmas right here, in this mid-century modern home. During his own childhood, shuffled back and forth between his parents, neither of whom really wanted the reminder of their failed first marriage, he'd rarely received a present or hung an ornament. But Vera adored Christmas, had turned into a whirling dervish of holiday cheer every year on the day after Thanksgiving, throwing tinsel around the house and singing carols in her off-key but delightful voice. Once the boys joined their fold, she made every year a special Christmas.

Jacob smiled, the ghosts of Christmases past frolicking through his memory. The year they had a gingerbread house-making contest and that dagblasted dog, that crazy Labrador named Benji, had eaten up every single one while they slept, and the boys woke them up Christmas morning in tears. The year Vera caved to the pressure in her church group to "put the Christ back in Christmas," only to end up on a last-minute shopping spree because her little boys deserved toys in addition to Jesus.

He remembered kissing her soft, full lips under the mistletoe year after year, as they evolved from youngsters fresh out of college to middle-aged empty nesters.

"Promise me you'll celebrate Christmas next year," Vera had said. The cancer had already ravaged her body, had shrunk her supple frame into that of a withered stick, but she looked beautiful to Jacob. He had tried to hold back his tears when he kissed her for what they both knew was their last Christmas together.

She had lasted another six months after Christmas until her body finally gave up.

The mistletoe was Jacob's one transgression in honoring Vera's wishes. He wanted to put it up, had even removed the tacky, glittering decoration from the storage bin, but he just couldn't do it. The snowmen, Santas, and reindeer cluttering the house were a different story—he looked at those and remembered the happy times, like when Caleb skateboarded into the tree, knocking it down, and they had to superglue the angel's head back on before Vera came home from her job at the bank. As a family, they had all laughed when Vera pointed out that their trickery hadn't worked since the head was now on *upside down*. And that plaster Santa, the goofy one in the swim trunks, bore witness to the wonderful trip to California they had taken after Hank's wedding.

But a mistletoe without a wife to kiss only heightened Jacob's loneliness. No, it didn't feel like Christmas without her, not even with her favorite holiday CD playing in the background.

Jacob refilled his mulled wine a few times while the fire died down. As he stared into the embers, he knew what he needed to do to feel close to her. He put on his jacket and placed the mistletoe in his pocket. It was a short drive to the cemetery.

No, he had had a little too much to drink. He should walk, even though it was late and a light snow was beginning to fall.

Vera would have loved it—it was going to be a white Christmas.

***

Jacob wished he'd had the sense to put on a hat. The few hairs left on his balding pate did a poor job of keeping out the chill. He gave a gentle squeeze to the mistletoe in his pocket and trudged up the hill, closer to his love.

When he finally reached the graveyard, Jacob marveled at its beauty. With the cleansing dusting of snow under the glow of a full moon, the elaborate tombstones looked positively regal. He smiled, glad he had forked out the lavish sum to buy a plot in the fancy burial ground against the protestations of his sons. Why *not* show the world how much he loved his wife?

The churchyard was hushed, quiet except for the low thrum of the wind. No other mourners joined Jacob at this late hour, though there was plenty of evidence of their love: poinsettias, small wrapped presents, even flasks of spirits. Jacob considered borrowing a swig to warm himself up, but he couldn't rationalize stealing from the dead, even if those decaying lips could no longer nurse a drink.

And there it was: the five-foot tall black marble Celtic cross to honor Vera's Irish heritage and religious devotion. It gleamed and beckoned him to come closer, a tribute to the beauty, kindness, and grace of his dear, departed wife.

"I miss you, my love," Jacob whispered, his lips trembling from cold. He had cut back on his visits after the boys told him it wasn't healthy, making it nearly two weeks without stopping by. "I brought the mistletoe."

He imagined Vera underneath the frozen, snow-covered ground. At her request, they had buried her in the dress she had planned to wear for their fortieth anniversary, which he had celebrated by himself this fall. She had splurged on it during their previous anniversary trip to Milan, buying it before the cancer diagnosis that changed everything. The undertaker needed to pin it back due to her weight loss, but Vera still appeared beautiful during her funeral.

Jacob wondered what she looked like now, six months later. Her limbs had barely contained any remaining flesh by the end of her life—how long would it cling to her bones? What about those once-lush lips? Did they continue to bear the imprint of decades' worth of his kisses?

He had paid extra for the fine engravings of their faces from their wedding day, those wrinkle-free kids with their whole lives ahead of them.

"Merry Christmas, baby," Jacob said, stooping down. With one arm, he held the mistletoe up over his head. He wrapped the other around the cross and pursed his lips into a kiss on the frigid marble likeness of his dead wife's face.

As he pulled himself up to his full height, he slipped on the slick snow. Trying to right himself, he grabbed the cross, which lurched forward toward his bulk.

***

Father Kowalski, who liked to clear his head with a brisk walk through the cemetery before mass, found him the next morning, Christmas Day. Jacob's body, crushed under the heavy marble cross, looked almost like a fallen snowman at first, for several more inches of snow had descended on his immobile form. When the priest realized what he was seeing, he rushed over to check for signs of life. Brushing off the blood-soaked snow, he grabbed Jacob's arm to check for a pulse.

Though Jacob's flesh was cold and lifeless, his heartbeat having ceased hours earlier, he continued to grip the mistletoe in his rigid hand, held over his head, ready for a kiss.

GETAWAY

Daylight faded along with Callie's strength, and her weary jog slowed to a halt. She could no longer see or hear the crashing waves of the Atlantic Ocean, but, as she gulped for more oxygen, she could smell it. Closing her eyes for a moment, she inhaled, taking in the brine beneath the stronger odor of rot.

It was time to leave.

***

When Meri called her out of the blue, Callie knew she needed something. It had been years with little contact, only the occasional text. And even that was usually just a GIF, something silly, inconsequential. Despite the voice of reason urging her to let the call go to voicemail, Callie answered.

"I have an idea," Meri whispered into the phone, no greeting or acknowledgment of the time that had passed. "Can you get away this weekend?"

Callie glanced at the piles of invoices on the desk of her home office and thought about the unread emails queued up in her inbox like lions waiting to be fed, each desperate for their meal. And if she ignored them, those questions and commands from her customers and investors, her jewelry design business wouldn't make it through the next quarter.

However, Callie couldn't resist the magnetic pull Meri had on her. Ever since second grade, when Meri, the new girl with the brassy Long Island accent, sat down across from her at the otherwise empty lunch table, Callie had been drawn into her web, available for her amusement or disposal, unable to shake the need for the bright light of Meri's presence.

"Where are we going?"

***

Barksdale Beach had gone out of fashion back when the most popular iron-on T-shirt designs were E.T. and the Care Bears, the town crumbling in equal measure with the erosion whittling away the already small beach. Callie remembered playing Skee-Ball at the arcade and buying cotton candy on the boardwalk when she was a kid, but, before she had entered her teen years, the tourists migrated to the surrounding Delaware beaches, bringing their money with them.

"I don't know about this," Callie said, pulling her car into the gravel parking lot. In her childhood, Harvest Hotel embodied grandeur and class; now, the paint-chipped siding and overgrown hedges of the establishment presented neglect and decay like the rest of the town.

"No one even knows us here anymore. It's fine," Meri said. "Your family moved away, what, when we were in college? And you know mine didn't even stay until high school graduation. This place is a ghost town."

Callie nodded. They were two women in their forties on a post-Christmas getaway, that was all, far removed from the teenagers questioned about the missing person back in the nineties. Nevertheless, grabbing her suitcase from the trunk, she paused. "We've talked about this. We both agreed to leave all this *behind*."

Meri's eyes locked with her own. "We never left it behind."

***

They hadn't made a reservation and didn't need to—the place was empty save for an old pickup truck in the parking lot, which Callie assumed belonged to the grizzled man behind the desk.

"We'll take—" she began.

"One room," Meri cut in.

"It's eighty dollars a night, even. Paid upfront." His watery eyes and downturned mouth remained unaffected by this surprise business.

"Just one night, then," Callie said, knowing that was all the Barksdale she could handle. When Meri made no move toward her purse, Callie paid in cash. Some things didn't change—Meri hadn't even given her gas money when Callie picked her up from the train station earlier, even though she'd driven all the way to New Jersey.

After depositing her duffel bag on the carpeted floor, Meri plopped down on one of the double beds. Compared to the hotel's decrepit façade, the room was surprisingly clean and homey, with thick, plush pillows and inviting comforters. "Not too bad," she said. "We might actually enjoy our stay here."

Callie pursed her lips, appraising her friend. In tight jeans and an oversized hoodie, with no makeup on and her hair tied into a casual ponytail, Meri didn't look much different than she had in high school. In contrast, the years manifested themselves on Callie: she had streaks of gray in her dark hair as well as wrinkles lining her forehead and surrounding her eyes. Ever since that afternoon at the beach, she had felt aged, and a flare of resentment at Meri ignited in her. "We're not here to enjoy ourselves. I thought you said that this is about honoring her. Saying goodbye, properly, since we didn't back then."

Meri rolled onto her stomach, childishly kicking her feet in the air. "You can't even say her name, can you? Say it, Callie. If we're really going to put this in the past and move on, you need to say her name. Dawn. Her name was Dawn, and we left her out there. Our friend."

"Her name was Dawn," Callie repeated, her voice hollow. She closed her eyes and let the memory wash over her.

***

The third member of their little gang, Dawn had moved to Barksdale the summer between eighth and ninth grade. Meri and Dawn both had jobs at the local Burger King and ended up bonding over being two of only a few female employees. Callie's parents wouldn't allow her to work until she was at least sixteen, saying she could babysit for extra money, but she rarely secured a gig. She spent long summer days reading and watching TV until Meri got off her shift and met her at the park, an equidistant spot between their houses. Soon enough, Dawn started tagging along. Callie was unsure at first, not really wanting to share Meri with anyone else, but Dawn was so sweet and good-natured that they melted into an easy camaraderie.

"I wish our beach hadn't fallen apart and that we still had a boardwalk," Meri grumbled, slouching on a swing, barely swaying. She sniffed her hair. "I hate smelling like meat and onions after my shift, and we're only making minimum wage. We'd have way cooler jobs if we worked on a boardwalk, but my mom said no way she'll drive me all the way to Rehoboth every day. It's not fair."

"There was a boardwalk in Barksdale?" From her place on the grass, bare legs akimbo, Dawn squinted up at her friends.

"Uh, yeah, it was, like, a huge deal when we were little," Callie said, smiling. "You would've loved it. You got the shit end of the stick coming to live now that it's gone. Barksdale used to be cool."

"I asked my mom if we could check out the beach, since it's so close to where our apartment is, but she said it's dangerous," Dawn said, rolling her eyes. "How can a beach be dangerous? I don't get it. And she hasn't even taken me to any of the other beaches, the nice ones, since we moved here, and it's almost time for school to start."

Not just school—*high* school. A rush of anxiety surged in Callie's veins as she considered the monumental step they were about to take.

Callie was never the one to suggest anything that broke the rules; that was always Meri's job. She and Dawn were the good girls who helped hold their friend back from bad decisions, like when that high school boy cat-called at them and Meri almost threw her Snapple bottle at him. But Dawn had become a close friend who deserved a treat. "How about we go check it out?" Callie's words, soft and breathy, crept out of her mouth like smoke.

"Really?" Meri asked. "You really want to go to Barksdale Beach even though we haven't gone since it shut down when we were kids and you have literally *never* agreed to go, no matter how many times I've asked you?"

Callie jumped off her swing. "If we leave now, we can get there in about thirty minutes, and that gives us about two hours to walk around before it gets dark and we have to go home."

On the way, Callie and Meri regaled Dawn with tales of the good old days when they were kids, back when they were members of a thriving beach community, their summers full of sand and salt water taffy. But that was before storms devastated the land, chipping away not only at the once expansive beach but also flooding and destroying several coastal properties, hotels included. And once the tourists stopped coming, the boardwalk businesses folded, unable to survive supported by the town alone. One by one, they closed up shop, leaving the boardwalk derelict. By that time, all efforts to secure funding to replenish the beach were denied by the federal government, and Barksdale Beach was sent off to pasture.

"My dad says that there are, like, junkies that go and shoot up out here," Meri said, a hint of tremor in her voice. "So let's just watch out for that and stick together."

The beach lay before them, littered with overgrown weeds and debris, nothing but a shell of the happy place Callie remembered from her childhood. Only a strip of sand remained to separate the dilapidated buildings from the ocean that had ravaged them.

"This place looks haunted," Dawn said after taking it all in. Her long, blonde hair blowing in the breeze and the sun glinting off her braces, she turned to smile at her friends. "I love it! This would be so scary at night, or, like, at Halloween! That old hotel might as well have a sign that says, 'Turn back now.'"

Staring at the rotting husk of the boarded-up Seafarers' Hotel, Callie remembered sneaking in to use the fancy bathroom as a kid only to get caught and chastised by a hotel employee. But no one could chase her away now. With its sagging roof and mottled exterior, the air of abandonment hung like a cloak on the building.

"What if we go in and explore?" she said. Callie didn't know this new daredevil version of herself and waited for the others to tell her how bad of an idea that was. *Surely* it wasn't safe.

But Dawn nodded, and Meri just shrugged. "Yeah, looks kinda cool. And you have to love the new decorating job." Meri pointed to a spray-painted penis gracing the side of the once pristine building.

"Should we walk along what's left of the beach first? Breathe in the salt air?" Callie asked, stalling. Even though it was her idea, she couldn't help but think of what might be lurking inside: spiders, rats, maybe even drug addicts, if Meri's dad could be believed.

Dawn jogged up to the front door. "There's a big padlock on here, but it's corroded or whatever, like green and crusty. Can we find a rock to see if we can break it?" she called out to them, her voice raised to compete with the roiling waves.

Callie glanced at Meri to see if she had similar doubts, but Meri's eyes were already darting along the beach, searching.

"It was *your* idea," Meri said, her voice low so only Callie could hear her. "We can't turn back now and disappoint Dawn. She's never even been here, so she deserves an adventure."

Even yards from the coastline, Callie's skin felt sticky from the ocean. She longed for darkness to fall so that she had an excuse to go home, to leave Barksdale Beach in the past where it belonged. But it *was* her idea to come here in the first place. Meri was right.

"I found something!" Meri cried out, holding up a smooth, gray stone about the size of her hand. She hurried over to Dawn.

Callie shuffled her feet in the pebbly sand, wincing from the scratch and scrape against her skin. She should have worn sneakers instead of sandals, but she hadn't planned on breaking and entering when she left her house that day.

"Ouch." Meri was already pounding at the lock when Callie caught up, but she paused to suck on her finger. "Hopefully I don't get tetanus from this old thing. Is that the one you get if old metal pokes you?"

"That lock can't be too old. This place has only been closed up for, like, six or seven years," Callie said, trying to be optimistic. Seeing the grime caked onto the building, it appeared to have been abandoned for far longer, decades, even.

"Let me try. Now that we're here, I really want in." Dawn grabbed the rock and began smashing it against the padlock, careful to avoid her fingers. It gave way after several tries, and Dawn wrenched the door open.

"God, what's that smell?" Meri crinkled her nose in disgust as the girls walked into the lobby.

"I think it's mold," Callie said, holding her tank top up over her nose and observing the green and black splotches painting the walls. "I think it's bad to breathe it."

"*You're* the one who wanted to come here," Meri reminded again, her voice challenging. "Let's go deeper in."

The two girls had fallen back into their roles, with Meri as the rule breaker and Callie the goody two-shoes. Callie started to say something but stopped when she saw the pleading in Dawn's eyes.

"We're definitely not the first people to come in here," Meri said, pointing to the empty beer cans and graffiti surrounding them.

"I wonder how they got in? Maybe somebody put the lock up later, to stop people?"

"I don't know, but let's hope no one's here now." Despite the mid-August heat, goosebumps formed on Callie's skin. It was chillier here, inside, away from the sun and closed in with the damp. She pressed the toe of her sandal into the soft, spongy carpeting and watched as it rose back up.

Dawn moved ahead. "I found how they got in! We could've saved ourselves some trouble if we walked around more." As her friends joined her, she pointed to the gaping hole in the side of the building. A single rotted board hung on, but the others had long since given up, pried off by mischievous hands or surges of the ocean, now lying in a heap underneath where a large picture window must once have been. "I sure would've loved to see this place in its glory. It's such a dump now." To annunciate her point, she gave a hearty smack to the exposed brick wall.

Weakened by the repeated onslaught of the Atlantic Ocean's salt and force, the mortar had eroded, and the wall began to cave in. Callie's "Run!" was drowned by a crash as a large chunk of wall tumbled inward toward Dawn.

Dawn's eyes bulged out, but her scream froze in her throat as bricks buried her in mere seconds.

A mountain of rubble lay in Dawn's place.

"Dawn? Can you hear me?" Callie's words croaked out in the quiet that followed. *Please let her be okay.* She looked over at Meri, who stood frozen in place, her arms stiff like tree branches, staring at the spot where their friend had been moments before. "We need to help her!"

Meri blinked her eyes, shook herself like a dog coming in from the rain, and fell to her hands and knees, grabbing and moving bricks. "Dawn! Are you okay?"

"We need to be careful or the rest of the wall might come down," Callie whispered, helping her, worried that even the sound of her voice could trigger another brick avalanche. But she wouldn't give up on her friend.

The girls worked in silence broken only by the sounds of their heavy breathing and occasional sobs. Their fun little adventure had transformed into a nightmare.

"There are lots of stories about caves collapsing, but the people are okay," Meri said, more to herself than Callie. "She could be okay. If she held up her arms, she could've blocked the bricks from hitting her head."

"She *has* to be okay," Callie said, not stopping in her chore even though the rough edges of the bricks tore at her fingertips. She didn't know what condition they'd find Dawn in, but she wanted to hold on to the hope that Dawn was alright. "I think I see something! Her foot!" She reached out and squeezed the big toe gently, Dawn's sandal having been lost underneath the ruins. It was faint, but she felt a twitch.

Finally, they unearthed their friend. Dawn's golden hair splayed out like sunbeams around her head, highlighting the red gash in her temple. A thin trickle of blood leaked out, running down the side of her face.

"Is she okay, do you think?" Meri asked, her voice thin and reedy. "Callie, tell me she's gonna be okay!"

Callie put her fingers on Dawn's neck, unsure what to do, but she knew that this was one way to check for proof of life. "I think I feel a pulse, so that means she's alive," she said. "But I don't know what we're supposed to do. We need to get help."

Meri bit her lip the way she always did when she concentrated. "Give me your bandana, and I'll put it around the wound. You know, to try and stop the bleeding? And I think we need to get her out of here before any more of that wall comes down."

"I don't think we're supposed to move someone who's injured, and we don't even know where all she's hurt," Callie said, taking the bandana off from around her head and handing it over anyway.

"She's gonna get a lot more injured, and so are we, if we stay here," Meri countered, fear and anger creeping into her tone. "And it was *your* stupid idea to come here in the first place! None of this should've happened today!"

"Shut up! I know! I freaking know, Meri! But what matters now is that we help her! We need to work as a team, okay?" Callie's blood boiled in frustration, not only at Meri for her outburst but for the vast unfairness of the situation. This shouldn't be happening to them. They only wanted a bit of fun.

After affixing the thin pink bandana as a makeshift bandage, Callie and Meri each grabbed one of Dawn's hands. Slowly, glaring at each other, they dragged Dawn's prone form away from the wreckage, through the hallway and lobby, and outside.

Panting with exhaustion, Callie surveyed her fallen friend. Dawn, small and childlike, lay on the sand motionless, peaceful except for the bloody bandana and purple bruises blooming on her pale skin like pansies. "She needs an ambulance. We can't carry her home. What do we do? We're, like, at least twenty minutes away from a phone. Should we split up? You stay with her and I'll run for help, or vice versa?"

Meri flopped onto the sand and cupped Dawn's face in her hand, ignoring Callie's questions. "I'm so sorry this happened to you, Dawnie."

"Meri. We need to figure something out. Now. Every moment we wait could be hurting her. This is *not* the time for you to be mad at me."

Meri tilted her head up at her friend, all self-assurance and swagger gone. "I'm scared. I don't know what to do."

"She'll die if we don't do anything!" The ocean roared behind Callie, the wind picking up in equal measure, whipping her loose hair in a tornado around her head. Hot tears streamed from her eyes, coating her cheeks. Callie sucked in a deep breath, trying to calm down as a torrent of emotions assaulted her. It wasn't the time for crying; she needed to take action. "You stay with her. I'll go. We still have daylight, at least, and I'll run. I'll call for help, and an ambulance will come. Just—just stay with her."

She removed her sandals and ran, traversing the beach and reaching the road, her bare feet slapping against the asphalt again and again. Her chest heaving, she allowed the tears to come, and they spilled out of her, mingling with her sweat. The wind continued to howl so that it almost sounded like her name.

"Callie!"

Callie stopped in her tracks, her raw feet blistering with pain, when she recognized Meri's voice.

"She's gone, Callie," Merri sobbed. "We were too close to the ocean, and a wave took her. I tried to hold on, but I couldn't. She's gone."

Callie gawked at her, uncomprehending. "But you were supposed to hold her. I was getting help. She was going to be okay. And I only left like ten minutes ago. I don't understand."

"It happened so fast. Then I started running to catch you before you told anyone." Meri walked closer, reaching out for an embrace, but Callie shook her off.

"We need to go back. Did you look for her? Your clothes are dry. Did you get in the ocean and try to find her?" Callie spoke in rapid, staccato sentences, her volume climbing.

"You're not listening! She's gone, Callie. Dead. Dawn is dead. There's nothing we can do for her." Meri wrapped her thin arms around herself and paused, taking a few slow, deep breaths. "We need to decide what we're going to say. We need to get our stories straight."

***

Decades later, walking toward Barksdale Beach on the cold but windless afternoon, Callie glanced sideways at her friend, remembering how they had fought on that fateful afternoon, how she had raged at Meri, actually slapping her hard in the face. But Callie came around to Meri's line of thinking.

Callie's actions—or lack thereof—weighed on her conscience, but she stuck to the story they'd concocted when the police came to question her. No, she hadn't hung out with Dawn that day; Dawn and Meri came to the park after their shift at Burger King, but Dawn said she had to take care of something and left right away. No, she didn't know what Dawn was doing, and she didn't know if Dawn was planning to run away. She and Meri never admitted to going to the beach, and Dawn's body was never found. She had simply disappeared without a trace.

Callie remembered Dawn's mother's pleas for any scrap of information. The poor woman appeared to age a decade in the weeks that followed, her eyes sinking back in her face, her golden hair, so much like her daughter's, becoming ratty and unkempt. And when the missing person posters went up all over town, Dawn's eyes stared out at Callie, accusing. *You left me*, they seemed to say.

Her grief at losing Dawn was genuine, at least. She didn't have to lie about *that*. She tried to keep her distance from Meri, both out of frustration that Meri let Dawn get taken by the ocean and from her own culpability. To be around Meri was to remember the last day all three of them spent together. But Meri was the only person who understood the crushing guilt she felt over what had happened to Dawn and how they couldn't save her, so the two girls continued their friendship, even if it was bound together by something darker than before.

When Meri's family moved away senior year of high school, Callie allowed the emotional distance between them to grow: a letter, phone call, or, later, a text, often with large lag times in between. They'd only gotten together twice over the many years, and both times involved other friends from high school, as well. Callie knew she and Meri would always be connected, but Meri's presence reminded her too much of Dawn's absence.

Meri broke the silence. "I think it'll be nice. We'll honor her, and then we'll both feel a little better. It was a terrible accident, but we were just kids who didn't know any better. It's not like we killed her. Any of the three of us could've died that day. We need to finally let it go and move on."

"I don't think it's our fault that she was hurt. We just should've handled it differently. We should've moved her to a safe place before I went for help. Or, at the very least, we should've told someone what happened. Maybe they would've found her and given her mom some answers. We could've saved her mom some of her pain, you know? Imagine never understanding why your only child ran away, always wondering if she's out there somewhere." Callie let out the sigh she'd been holding in. She'd had this conversation in her head over and over, but this was the first time in years she'd talked about it directly with Meri.

Callie imagined herself in a courtroom, waiting to be charged, Dawn's now elderly mother a picture of fury and grief. "Sometimes I wonder if we should tell, just fess up and see what happens to us for the lies we told when we were minors. Maybe *nothing* would happen."

"I don't think it helps Dawn if we destroy our lives. I mean, look at the two of us. Forty-two years old and neither of us has ever been married or had a long-lasting relationship. At this point, we probably won't get the chance to have kids, and neither of us ended up getting our dream jobs or anything. Haven't we been punished enough? Maybe it's karma," Meri said. "Maybe none of the three of us got to really grow up. Dawn died, and we became stuck."

Stuck. The word lodged itself in Callie's brain, a tight, uncomfortable fit. "Maybe you're right," she said, her mind cataloging her many failures over the years: the starts and stops at grad school; the business ventures that never quite worked out; the men she'd kept at a distance until they finally took the hint and left on their own.

A lone car drove by, the first they'd seen since they left Harvest Hotel. There was nothing out here anymore, not really—just the bad memories. The beach had further diminished, leaving the space between the ocean and the road a jungle of weeds and abandoned buildings. Callie closed her eyes and tried to summon the happy images from days at the beach with her family from her childhood, but all she could remember was Dawn: the tinkle of her laugh, the way she scrunched up her nose, the cock of her eyebrow if she was unsure of something. When it came down to it, she could count her friendship with Dawn in weeks. But those weeks, short as they were, had formed a lasting impression strengthened by what happened.

Meri picked her way over broken bottles and sticks, heading closer to the old Seafarers' Hotel where the accident had occurred. "Do you think we should go inside?"

"Geez, Meri, of course not! It wasn't safe then and definitely isn't now! Let's go around to the other side, where the wall collapsed. We can say goodbye there."

They walked around the building, finding the slumping wall easily enough. Callie wondered if any part of Dawn was left behind inside, a scrap of her clothes or the stain of her blood. But, based on the proximity of the ocean, high tide had probably swum through the hotel enough times to wash it all away.

Meri sat on the ground cross-legged and began rummaging in her bag. "I don't know if we should wait until nightfall, but I think it might get too dangerous to find our way back, and maybe too cold. First thing, we have to light this candle, and then we'll say what we remember about her and tell her we're sorry for what happened." She pulled out a printout of Dawn—the photograph from the missing person poster she must have found online—as well as a tall, thick, red candle, which she placed on top of the paper, pushed into the dirt, and lit with a match.

Meri closed her eyes. "Dawn, if you can hear me, I want you to know how much I miss you. We didn't know each other long, but you were one of my closest friends. Ever. I miss your smile and how you always sang along to the music when we were at work even when it was cheesy. *Especially* when it was cheesy. I'm so sorry this awful wall crushed you and that the ocean tore you away from me. I hope you can forgive me for not being able to hold on to you. *I vocare te.*"

A thunder of waves broke behind them as the wind picked up. The candle snuffed out, and drops of the thick, viscous, red wax splashed onto Dawn's white paper face.

Callie, who had bowed her head in deference as Meri spoke, snapped up her neck. Her words tumbled out as her body perceived the change in atmosphere, the hairs on the back of her neck rising even under her heavy winter jacket. "What did you just say? What's actually happening here? I thought you said we were going to say some nice things to remember her! What did you *do*, Meri?"

"It's a summoning spell," Meri replied. "I thought we could have real closure if we got a chance to actually say goodbye. If she comes to us."

"What the actual fuck? I didn't sign on for this! I don't believe in that stuff, but I also don't like it. What's wrong with you? I'm leaving." Callie stood up and brushed the sand off her jeans. Even though she claimed not to believe in it, the timing of the mounting wind and raging ocean seemed like more than a coincidence.

Meri's hand shot up, grabbing Callie's wrist. "Let me light the candle again. You need to talk to her, too. Maybe she'll come to us then."

Callie looked in horror at the woman she called a friend but was more like a stranger. Meri stared back at her but also through her—her eyes had taken on a sort of vacancy that sent a shiver down Callie's spine.

Something was *not* right.

"We need to leave, Meri. Grab your bag, and let's go. We can go to a church or something tomorrow before we leave town, and we'll light a candle for her. You know, memorialize her. But we are *not* doing this," Callie begged.

Another sound filled the air along with the deafening waves and tempestuous wind: a trill of soft, girlish laughter.

A creature that was once Dawn poked its head out from the hotel, through the open space of the crumbling brick wall, and spoke in a wet, garbled voice. "That was sweet, Meri. How could I *not* come? And it's about time you came to visit me!"

As Callie regarded the lank blonde hair and bloated, dappled skin of her onetime friend, she tasted bile. This couldn't be happening, yet it was. Meri's hand released her wrist just as Callie tried to pull her to her feet.

Meri stood, walked closer to the ghoul, and reached out, extending her fingers. "You came," she said, her voice joyful. "Callie, she's here. She forgives us for leaving her."

Dawn opened her mouth to expose two rows of sharp, pointed teeth, which she curved into a smile. "Who said anything about forgiveness? Let me show you how a friend can hold on to another friend." She clasped onto Meri's outstretched hand and yanked, drawing her through the opening as if she weighed almost nothing.

Callie started running away from the sound of Meri's ragged, agonizing screams, which lasted only a few seconds before they stopped. Pumping her arms and legs, Callie kept going, just like she had back then, sweat beading on her forehead and underneath her layers. She focused on nothing but putting distance between herself and whatever was left of her two friends at Barksdale Beach.

***

Later, on the drive home to Pennsylvania, Callie thought about what might happen next. She hadn't done anything wrong, after all. *Meri* was the one who cast that summoning spell, not her. Meri brought it on—whatever *it* was—all by herself. But if anyone asked Callie about what happened to Meri, they might think that she was responsible. She needed to retrace her steps.

She'd returned her key, muttering an excuse that something had come up and she couldn't stay the night. She offered no explanation for the absence of her traveling companion, and the old man wouldn't find any trace of either woman if and when he bothered servicing the room; Callie had taken Meri's duffel with her and wiped down all the surfaces they might have touched. She hadn't given the proprietor her driver's license or even written down her name—he had no idea who she was or where she had gone.

There *was* the matter of a cell phone record. Meri had texted and called Callie before their trip, so it was possible someone might place the two of them together, but would anyone bother? Meri's parents were dead, and she had been estranged from her younger sister for a number of years. Last Callie knew, Meri was working for a temp agency, so it wasn't likely she had close colleagues who might show concern.

Maybe no one would notice Meri's disappearance. Maybe no one would care.

Callie supposed she should feel grief for the loss of her friend, as well as fear and revulsion for the violence she witnessed that day, but a cold sense of calm engulfed her. Whether she meant to or not, Meri was the one who had lost her grip on Dawn, and Dawn had returned to exact her revenge. There was a strange kind of symmetry, really.

It had nothing to *do* with Callie. It was tragic, but it wasn't her fault. Meri was right, as it turned out: Revisiting Barksdale Beach had allowed Callie to make a sort of peace with what had happened to Dawn all those years ago.

Callie had driven in silence for the past hour, trying to collect her thoughts, but she felt her strength returning. She flipped on the radio to her favorite nineties station and sang along with Lenny Kravitz's "Fly Away."

She drove on, leaving Barksdale Beach and all the secrets it held in her wake.

I'LL SLEEP TOMORROW

Tim shut his laptop, a wide grin spreading over his face. *Tenure, baby!* He was nearly there after all this time: those grueling years earning his PhD in archeology as he scraped by on his measly graduate assistant stipend, eating Cup Noodles and frozen pizza; the panic-inducing search across the country for a tenure-track job in a field he was told was dying; the four plus years since then navigating office politics, dealing with student problems exacerbated by the pandemic, and, of course, trying to publish and present his research. But now, *now* his hard work would pay off. Tenure was his for the taking.

A quick glance at the clock: 12:15 in the morning, and his first class was at nine a.m. Removing his glasses, Tim rubbed his eyes and imagined what his mother would say if she knew he was at the office this late once again. But she didn't understand this world of academia. A third-grade teacher, she had been thrilled when Tim declared, at the tender age of nineteen, that he wanted to be an educator, but she was fully unprepared for the hoops through which he would have to jump, the wear and tear he would put on mind and body.

"You're working too hard," she had said at Christmas after pinching his waist in search of non-existent fat. Tim had never fully regained his appetite after that bout of dysentery from the summer dig in Belize, but he'd helped uncover an important Mayan artifact that would justify a future grant. The article was finished and accepted for publication, and he was presenting a paper on it in Portugal after spring break, fully-funded, so those few weeks of misery were well worth it.

His mom didn't get it, though, and kept nagging. "Take it easy on yourself. Focus on your health more: Eat, and make sure you're getting enough sleep."

"I'll sleep tomorrow," Tim said, even though he knew it rankled his only living parent. "Things will calm down soon after this."

But they didn't, not really. There were papers to grade, lectures to prepare, committee work to complete, students to advise, and then the process of tenure itself: the long narratives to prove his competence in teaching, scholarship, and service; the sorting, cataloging, and documenting of faculty and course evaluations, conference abstracts, transcripts, and publications.

Even his department chair, an older woman named Brenda who reminded Tim of his mom, had said something to him when she caught him in the office late on a Saturday. "You'll be fine, Tim. You'll definitely get tenure. It's time to start saying no to things and taking better care of yourself. Go home and get some rest, or get a drink with a friend or something. You need some balance in your life."

Brenda may have had good intentions, and she'd been a wonderful mentor when Tim was a new hire trying to decipher the ins and outs of the job, but she didn't get it, or at least didn't remember, not from her lofty place as a tenured full professor. The thought of not receiving tenure, of needing to go back on the job search, terrified Tim to the core. He'd heard about a friend from grad school, a year ahead of him, who'd been rejected, and now he was living in his parents' basement and working at Home Depot, all those years of education and toil for naught.

And Blackthorn University had been good to him. Sure, it wasn't an R1 university, just a small liberal arts college in rural Pennsylvania, but he loved it there, from the old stone buildings to the graceful, drooping trees that covered campus and blanketed the sidewalks in rust and golden leaves every autumn. His colleagues, mostly good people, often complimented his achievements and offered their help if he needed it. Tim's students, many of whom ended up in his class to fill an elective, were overall friendly and attentive. Once in a while, he lit a fire in one of them, opening their eyes to the magic and mystery of an ancient civilization. To his delight, recognizing his young, excited self in them, he'd even convinced some to become archaeology majors. No, he couldn't bear the thought of being rejected for tenure and having to leave Blackthorn.

Yet here Tim was, tenure manuscript complete, two days before the deadline, 73 pages not even counting the supplemental documents, everything uploaded and submitted to the Dropbox. All he had to do was turn in his signature page to the president's office the next day. Even though everything else for tenure had gone paperless after Covid, and it would have been easy enough to obtain electronic signatures from his department chair and committee members, the president liked the tradition of having applicants turn in a physical copy to his office.

Tim yawned and gathered his belongings. He decided to leave his laptop—there wasn't time between now and his first class to get anything else done, and maybe, just maybe, he'd finally get to relax after this. He could write that letter of recommendation on his break between classes the next day. If he earned tenure, he could apply for promotion to associate professor the following year; some of his grad school friends at other institutions were applying for both at the same time, but Blackthorn didn't offer that option. In the meantime, once he submitted the sheet, it would all be in the university tenure committee's and eventually the president's hands, so maybe he deserved a break.

Not yet. He needed to turn in that sheet, a simple act that still felt like one more task to cross off his never-ending to-do list. If he took it home with him now, he could drop it off first thing in the morning before class, not even stopping at his office. Then he'd have fulfilled *all* his tenure obligations.

Looking at the crisp, white paper with its scrawled signatures, one of which was smudged, Tim thought back on his journey to reach this point and sighed in contentment. He grabbed a folder to keep it safe and headed out of his office.

***

The full moon shone over the desolate campus as Tim walked to his car in the huge, now vacant lot. Mere hours from now, thousands of students, faculty, and staff, bundled up against the frigid January chill, would scurry about and bring the campus back to life from its slumber with laughter, conversation, and general hustle and bustle. In the wee hours of the morning, though, the only sounds disrupting the silence were Tim's footsteps on the pavement and the howling, keening wind.

Tim opened his jaws wide for another deep yawn as tiredness overtook his body. Thank goodness his apartment was right off campus—he didn't want to doze off at the wheel. If he were lucky, if he could wind down his mind and fall asleep right away once he went to bed, he could get maybe six hours before he needed to ready himself for the day. Placing his folder on top of his car and holding his empty travel mug with his other hand, he reached in his pocket for his keys.

That's when a gust of wind hit him hard in the face, jolting him awake and blowing the folder off the car. Tim groaned in frustration, stretching out his long arm to the ground as the playful gale somersaulted the folder away from his grasp and up in the air, higher and higher.

Running now, Tim breathed hard as he commenced the chase across the parking lot. He *needed* that folder with its precious cargo, his signature page. He felt like he was on a prank show, like some unseen jokester had attached his folder to a string and was jerking it around for laughs as he, hapless fool, bumbled along. How was he, Assistant Professor Timothy Chandler, PhD, a pretty good guy all around, the sufferer of this misfortune when all he wanted to do after a long day was to go home and rest? He didn't deserve this.

"You've got to be kidding me," he said aloud as the folder sailed beyond the orange and white barricade blocking off the construction site. Blackthorn always seemed to be beautifying something old or building something new, and this time it was a grandiose dorm that, when completed, would house almost three hundred students in state-of-the art suites. While this seemed a little ambitious considering that many of Blackthorn's population came from middle or low-income backgrounds, Tim had seen the floorplans and had to admit the building would be sure to impress prospective students and their parents.

As he squeezed through the barricade, past the orange plastic safety net, plastic cones, and warning signs, he didn't give a rat's ass about that damn building's magnificence. He just wanted his folder, which finally stilled its shenanigans, resting on the edge of the foundation site. How lucky that it hadn't been whisked into the depths!

Tim picked up the folder and turned on his heels to head back, determined not to lose to the wind this time. But in that swift motion, his mind homed in on the folder and nothing else, his body exhausted with lack of sleep and improper nutrition, he misjudged his balance and slid down the steep dirt wall of the excavation site.

Some self-preservation instinct must have fired in his brain, for Tim leaned into the fall and reached the bottom with scarcely a tumble. He set down his folder and empty travel mug, stood, and brushed the dirt off his pants and the monstrous puffy jacket his mother had given him for Christmas. Under the moonlight's glow, he estimated maybe ten, twelve feet of dirt walls looming over him.

"Unbelievable," he muttered. He tested the wall, digging in his fingernails with both hands and attempting a foothold with the big toes within his loafers, but, in the cold of the night, the earth was solid, unyielding. Again and again he endeavored with the same result.

He could call campus police. It would be embarrassing, and he might even get in trouble, but he'd need to swallow his pride. Yet, when he reached into his pocket for his phone, it wasn't there, having fallen during his mad dash across campus to catch his folder.

Tim sat on the ground, placed his head in his hands, and wept. He wasn't a crier by nature, but he was so damn tired. He didn't like to be a pessimist, though. He'd be fine—it was cold out, but not to the point that he'd freeze to death, and the construction workers would likely be there by eight a.m. if not earlier. He'd seen them countless times in the morning, already hard at work when he hadn't yet drunk his first coffee.

There'd be some awkwardness, but they'd help him out, and maybe he'd even make it to his class in time. Surely he wouldn't get in too much trouble after he explained about the signature page. If it went all the way to the dean, she'd understand, wouldn't she? No one had been denied tenure for trespassing on a construction site with a valid reason, had they?

There was nothing to gain by stressing about the consequences, so Tim took a few deep breaths and ended his pity party. He pulled the hood of his jacket over his head, tucked himself into a corner, and curled into a fetal position to conserve warmth. As he fell asleep, his last thought was that he'd laugh about this someday, how he wanted tenure so badly that he fell into a construction site.

***

Vince and Chuck were first to arrive that morning. They'd worked countless jobs at Blackthorn in the last two decades and were known to be dependable, but Chuck's son, Bryce, hadn't shown.

Vince looked at his phone. "Where's he at? It's ten after already. Mike's gonna have our asses if we don't get started."

"He didn't come home last night. Again. I told him he'll lose this gig if he doesn't get his act together, just like he screwed up his last two jobs." Chuck sighed and looked away, not wanting his buddy to see the pain in his eyes.

But Vince understood, having a couple of ne'er do well kids of his own. "Look. Let's get started. I know we contracted for a three-person job, but it's like thirty degrees today, so it's gonna take a while to set. We can control the chute together, and then we'll stop it after a bit and jump into the pit and spread it. We're pros. We got this." Vince placed his gloved hand on Chuck's shoulder, a sign of support. "Mike doesn't need to know a thing, and hopefully your boy'll show up before anyone misses him."

Chuck nodded in acquiescence, clamping his jaw to avoid any show of emotion, and the two set to work.

***

When Tim awoke to the assault of cold, wet cement, he opened his mouth to scream, but a glob of the concoction went straight down his throat, rendering him mute. He coughed and spluttered, flailing his arms and legs about, trying to free himself from the heavy, sticky prison in which his body was encased, but it was useless. Pinned to the ground, flat on his back, Tim's frail, tired body was trapped. As the cement covered him, its weight bearing down, suffocating, he realized that this was it. He wouldn't earn tenure, not this year and not ever. His final thoughts were of unfinished business.

***

By the time Vince and Chuck climbed down the ladder to begin the leveling and smoothing process, Assistant Professor

Timothy Chandler, PhD, had expired. Vince thought he saw a bump in the corner, but a few swipes of his screed reoriented the cement right over the thin professor who worked too hard and sometimes forgot to eat.

None of Tim's colleagues or students, certainly not his poor mother, would ever discover Tim's fate. No one knew why he had submitted those tenure materials at just past midnight but never made it to his car. His phone, discovered in the parking lot and turned in to campus police the next day, offered no help.

Maybe someday, hundreds of years in the future, a budding archeologist might dig about the ruins of a liberal arts college in rural Pennsylvania and find the remains of one young professor and whatever was left of his possessions—tenure signature page, glasses, and travel coffee mug—and form a hypothesis about work/life balance in the 2020s.

AFTERWORD: HOW I MADE THE SAUSAGE AND OTHER SPOILERS

In my real job as an English professor, I'm constantly asking my students to reflect on their work, and I feel the need to do a bit of this here. I teach both composition and creative writing, and the two are wildly different to me. In my comp classes, one of my roles is demystifying the process of writing for students as they work to build their fluency, yet creative writing *can* be a little magical. Back when I was writing up research studies, while it was always a tremendous effort, I put in the time and got the job done. I racked my brain and figured out the problems. I was proud of this work, but it never really felt like creation—it was more of a process that I followed. I filed the necessary permissions, read previous research studies that informed my own, took tons of notes, created my own research questions, etc. There was much to be done before I sat down to do any writing. I don't know how someone can do much research without an incredible amount of planning.

With my creative writing, though, I've sat down to write with a single or vague idea and have felt the words flow out of me, not knowing quite where I'm going until I get there. It's not that I start with a blank slate when I sit down—I'll have an idea, and my brain will work at the story while I'm doing other things like washing the dishes; it's like having a poppyseed stuck between my teeth, and my tongue finds itself working the area while I'm not even thinking about it. While this isn't my writing process for a novel, it's worked for me in a short story. I've had times where I've stepped away from my computer shaken by the dark turn a story took. When I wrote "Crawl Space," for example, I actually closed my laptop and walked away, horrified by the actions of my character. To me, it's a bit mystical when the characters take over.

Friends have often told me that I *seem* normal enough, but then they read my writing, and they tell me (often with weird looks on their faces) they don't know where I get all these dark ideas. Along with that elusive magic comes a lot of discipline—time sitting in front of my laptop and trying to write something, anything, even when the muse doesn't seem to have time for me. I look for inspiration everywhere and probably turned to horror in the first place since my mind often imagines the worst-case scenario of a situation. One quality that each of my stories carries is a kernel of real life, something to make the mayhem that ensues a little more plausible. Here's how these stories came into existence.

"Keeper of Corpses": Ever since I met someone who told me interesting anecdotes about working in a funeral home, I wanted to write something involving the preparation of the dead, but my early research into mortuary practice made me wary of being able to pull off the intricacies involved. As a teenager, I worked in a nursing home, though, and that made me take this other avenue (even though I was a dietary aide and not ever near dead bodies). I came up with the title and thought I'd just write a story of a shy nurse who prepared bodies, but then I thought about another way she could be the keeper of corpses… and I simply couldn't stop her from her vengeance.

"Soothsayer": As a child, I listened as my father told me Greek myths which included my namesake, the Trojan princess cursed by Apollo to foresee a future that no one would believe. Since it would be awkward to give a story my own first name, I turned to *Julius Caesar*, one of my favorite plays to teach when I taught high school, for help with a title. After writing this, I take the stairs as often as I can.

"Untenanted": The first line for this story popped into my head when I couldn't sleep one night, so I had to write the rest to find out what happened. If I had found out how to "travel" when stuck in fabric stores as a child, I'm pretty sure I would have tried it.

"Budget Wine Tour": At a winery in Chile, I sat in a below-ground, cavernous room at a beautifully decorated table to enjoy a tasting. While my own trip worked out far better than Derek's and

Clara's, I couldn't help but think what a perfect setting it was for a horror story.

"And They Marched On": A massive understatement about me is that I hate crowds. About half of this story is nonfiction; you can guess which half.

"Skin Deep": There's far too much importance placed upon women's appearances. There—I said it! Poor Jean.

"From the Sea to the Sea": On a visit to Cabo San Lucas almost twenty years ago, I was walking by the ocean with my Skechers sandals in my hand when a wave grabbed them away from me. Even though we had been warned about the ocean's strength at that section of the beach, my instinct was to turn and fight for my shoes. Though I only stepped forward a foot or two, a wave came back and grabbed me, pulling me from shore and slamming me into the ocean floor. Despite a summer as a lifeguard, despite growing up with a pool in my backyard and spending long days treading water, I couldn't get a single breath. Whenever I managed to get my head above water and open my mouth, ready to snag a breath of air, the angry ocean pulled me down again. The only thought worse than "I really might drown" was when I saw my daughter, days away from her eighth birthday, notice what was happening with horror etched into her face as she ran closer to the water. I worried that the ocean might take us both.

Luckily, some amazing teenager, a far stronger swimmer than me, also noticed my distress and saved me. He managed to get my shoes, too, though I have no idea how. He refused my offer of money and left me grateful but shaken on the beach.

When I started this particular story, all I knew was that my main character would drown. I started with the setting in Mexico, but I had several other stories set in Spanish-speaking countries and needed something different. My subconscious must have been at work, for I only realized how very Greek the theme of the story was after I had set it there.

"(In)termina(b)l(e)": I don't have much in common with Jackson, thank goodness, but we both hate airports. On a trip to South America a month or so before I wrote this, I thought to myself how my own version of hell might involve being stuck at an airport for eternity. I already had the story in mind when a very terrifying event occurred: While sitting in my own backyard, having a drink with my friend Ailien and my husband, we heard a loud crack as a tree branch broke above us. One of us yelled, "Run!" The weight of the branch broke another one, and the combined weight plummeted to my sturdy Adirondack chair, breaking it—smashing the area where my head had been seconds before. What's really freaky is that Ailien had just mentioned the movie *Final Destination*. The whole experience was too close for comfort, but I knew I had to immortalize it in a story.

"A Gift for Avery": I typed up the original version of this story, "The Doll," on an Apple IIe computer for my seventh grade English class. I rewrote it a couple of times over the years and received an important rejection for it; the editor told me he enjoyed my writing but that I hadn't done enough in the story to make it different from all the others before it. This sent me on the path of exploring horror tropes, which I studied while working on my MFA, and I ended up editing a multiauthor volume of horror scholarship with Vernon Press, *No More Haunted Dolls: Horror Fiction that Transcends the Tropes*. As much as tropes can work as a staple in horror, and as much as we expect certain conventions from the genre, we need something different, something more than a shiny new coat of paint. "A Gift for Avery" is my attempt to add some depth to the haunted doll cliché.

"Itch": This story is brought to you by mosquito bites. I received so darn many this past summer that I scratched away my flesh and started to imagine a larger evil residing beneath my skin.

"Crawl Space": Yes, the second story in this collection where bodies are buried in someone's basement! As a child, I had recurring dreams where I found dead bodies hidden away in the basement, and I have a general aversion to this area of the house. I wrote this story before "Keeper in Corpses" and based the idea off of two nuggets of truth: I have a dog who has been labeled as difficult by people, and I have a super creepy crawl space in my house (no dead bodies, though). In an unfortunate prophecy, after I wrote this story, my dog killed a rabbit which ran into the yard, and I had to dispose of its body. I obviously did not bury it in my crawl space!

I've long been fascinated (and terrified) by people who make an impulsive, terrible decision to avoid getting in trouble and allow things to spiral out of control. It was bad enough that Jared disposed of Cindy as he did, but what really got under my skin was the way he talked to her afterward.

"The Mirror": As a child, I had a huge mirror in my room, and I used to run past it at night before climbing up to my loft to go to bed just in case something reached out. There's something nefarious about mirrors at nighttime.

"The Cigarette-Mouthed Man": I'm no fan of cigarette smoke, and I had a nightmare about this guy.

"Matka Loves You": In a way, this piece, originally written in screenplay form for my MFA program, is another take on the haunted doll trope. In this case, it's the woman, not the doll, who's haunted.

"Under the Apple Tree": I had a seed of an idea of this story for years—a simple man who was wrongly accused of killing a child. I find this story incredibly sad.

"Tunnel Vision": This started as a creative nonfiction piece about my issues with driving. Sadly, I have major driving anxiety. Happily, that is the only thing the narrator and I have in common (well, and maybe a bitchy college roommate).

"Night School": I used to teach high school and have met every single type of misbehaved student, and I therefore have a slew of classroom management techniques up my sleeves. While I consider myself well-versed in making progress with students whose troubles manifest in acting out, there were a few over the years where nothing I did got through to them. I'm also not a vampire, though.

"Glitch in the System": As an educator, people like Alice are the bane of my existence, always making excuses for why her students aren't learning, refusing to take any responsibility. Even if not for the awful and evil incident in her past, I would still hate her for coasting her way to retirement instead of trying to work with students.

"When the Truth Comes Crashing Down": Sitting at a bar with friends as a huge elk head crashed down on the (thankfully) empty table beside us, not actually causing any damage but scaring the hell out of all of us, I knew I needed to put that in a story.

"Run!": A number of years ago, my younger sister, our husbands, and I ran in a zombie 5K, and it was terrifying. I knew the "zombies" were actors, but my terror felt real. When I swam across a stream, I knew that no one would be submerged under the water to pull me down, but I was still afraid it would happen. After the "zombies" stripped me of my life flags, they left me alone, unlike in the story. Also, my sister and I have much better husbands.

"House of Screams": One of the oldest stories in this collection, it's pretty tropey, but I hope you found it campy and fun.

"Not a Cat Guy": This is the first piece of fiction I wrote in first-person from the perspective of a man, and early readers told me it sounds extremely different from my voice, and that's exactly what I hoped. I'm a bit of Jason's opposite, as I most definitely AM a cat person. I wrote most of it longhand during jury duty since I couldn't have my phone or a computer on me, and I hoped that I'd be forced to get some writing done during my long day of waiting to see if I'd get called. It worked! I walked away with $12 for my service and most of this short story.

"Christmas Market Massacre": Inspired by a quick but memorable trip to a Zurich Christmas market, this story contains, in my opinion, the most despicable villain out of all my stories. Even though Amanda was assuredly a mean girl and no true friend to Stacey, she didn't deserve to die, and nor did the rest of the innocent victims.

"Hungry Christmas": Several years ago, I made a poor decision to go outlet shopping on my birthday despite threats of a snowstorm. It's not supposed to snow in mid-November in Pennsylvania! By the time we made it to the outlets, they were closing, and we began a perilous trek home in a blizzard that should have taken one hour but took six. I am happy to state that things turned out better for us than they did for Henry and Cole, but it was horrible. At least it served as a point of realism in this story!

"Together for Christmas": No personal connection here, but I've heard real life stories about accidents like this.

"Getaway": Every summer, I stay in Dewey Beach with close friends I made when I lived in Delaware and taught high school English. I'm pleased to say that no one ever gets left behind.

"I'll Sleep Tomorrow": If you've ever wondered what it's like to be a professor going up for tenure, here's a glimpse.

ABOUT THE AUTHOR

Cassandra O'Sullivan Sachar is a writer and associate English professor in Pennsylvania who teaches creative writing and composition classes. A career educator, she previously worked as an English teacher in Delaware public schools. She holds a Doctorate of Education with a Literacy Specialization from the University of Delaware and an MFA in Creative Writing with a focus on horror fiction from Wilkes University. She has traveled to more than fifty countries but also loves being at home with her husband, rescue dog, and a reasonable number of cats. She is the author of the novel *Darkness There but Something More*. Visit her website at cassandraosullivansachar.com.

PUBLICATION HISTORY

The stories listed first appeared in the following publications: "Untenanted," *Wyldblood Magazine* (2023); "Budget Wine Tour," *Ink Stains: A Dark Fiction Literary Anthology*, ed. N. Apythia Morges (2022); "From the Sea to the Sea," *The Chamber Magazine* (2023); "A Gift for Avery" and "The Mirror," PsychoToxin Press (2023); "The Cigarette-Mouthed Man," *Soulmate Syndrome: Doomed Romance Fictions Vol. 1*, ed. Rasiika Sen and Parth Sarathi Chakraborty (2023); "Matka Loves You," *patrickmcnulty.ca* (2023), "Tunnel Vision," *Rosette Maleficarum* (2023); "Under the Apple Tree," *Corvus Review* (2022); "Night School," *White Cat Publications* (2023); "When the Truth Comes Crashing Down," *The Pine Cone Review* (2022); "Run!" (originally published as "Running for My Life"), *The Stygian Lepus* (2023); "House of Screams," *The Horror Zine* (2023); "Not a Cat Guy," *Dark Horses Magazine* (2024); "Christmas Market Massacre," *Blood Moon Rising Magazine* (2023); "Glitch in the System," *The Horror Zine* (2023); "Hungry Christmas," *Eerie Christmas 2*, ed. D. Kershaw and S. Jade Path (2021); "Together for Christmas," *Tales from the Moonlit Path* (2021); "I'll Sleep Tomorrow," *Pennsylvania English* (2024).

The rest of the stories are original to this collection.

MORE CHILLS FROM VELOX BOOKS

SPIRALING DOWN
DISTURBING HORROR STORIES BY MICHAEL MARKS

PLASTIC FACES
"STRIKING, BITING, AND WICKED. YOU WON'T WANT TO MISS THIS COLLECTION."
UNSETTLING STORIES BY MARTA ABROMAITYTE

THESE LONELY PLACES
STORIES THAT ARE GUARANTEED TO ENTERTAIN

I'VE DONE THIS BEFORE
"TRULY SPECIAL"
A BARRAGE OF NIGHTMARES BY RYAN MAJOR

OUR DARK THOUGHTS
A COLLECTION OF TERRIFYING TALES
KYLE HARRISON

IRON MAIDENS
"AN EXCELLENT COLLECTION OF HORRORS"
TWISTED TALES OF KILLER WOMEN
SARAH JANE HUNTINGTON

STRANGE TALES OF THE MACABRE
TALES BY E. REYES

FACE DOWN IN THE GRAVE
"A GREAT LITTLE COLLECTION OF THE BIZARRE [AND] MACABRE."
SINISTER TALES BY THOMAS O.

TRIPPING OVER TWILIGHT
DARK TALES BY T.W. GRIM

MORE CHILLS FROM VELOX BOOKS

Made in the USA
Middletown, DE
23 March 2025